# Sunfire!

I0616857

## By EDMOND HAMILTON

*He was walking in the pine grove, with the resinous smell of the trees in his nostrils. Once he had met a smell vaguely like it, far away from Earth. Forget about that, a voice said in his mind, but he would never forget.*

EVERYTHING in the old house seemed just the same as it had been before he went to space.

It was incredible, thought Hugh Kellard, standing in the front hall and looking around the silent, sunlit rooms, how little it had changed. The life was gone out of it now, all the people and voices and the comings and goings when his grandfather still lived and he had visited here. But that had been long ago, and he was amazed that so much remained still untouched.

"Like travelling into the past," thought Kellard, "to come back to this part of Earth."

He was tired, in body and mind and nerve, and he stood for a while, just staring. The agent who cared for the old place had let him in and gone away, and there was not a sound in the house. He walked into the living room where his grandfather's desk still stood beneath a window, and looked out. The window faced northward, along the California coastal cliffs that run north along Morro Bay to Big Sur. The Pacific foamed and surged against the huge broken stones beneath the cliffs, and the hills, somber now with a tinge of autumn, shouldered massively up toward the east from the cliff road. It all looked as lonely as ever, no other houses in sight but this gray, weather-beaten house that had faced the sea-wind and the sea-fog for over a hundred years.

Kellard walked back along the hall. On its walls still hung the ornately framed family photos, which his grandfather had stubbornly kept in place. His great-grandfather, and his great--aunt something, and all the rest of them, on back into the shadows. They were all there, they had not been touched, nothing in the house had been touched, just as his grandfather's will had enjoined. Keep the old house, he had said. Some of the family will be back some day.

The old man had been right, he thought. One of the family had come back at last, one who had roamed farther than almost anybody on Earth.

"But that's all done with," he told himself. "Here I am, and here I stay. I'm through with space."

HE started through the rooms, opening windows, letting in light and air. The furniture was faded and old-fashioned, but the place was not dusty, the agent had seen that it was kept in shape. Kellard picked one of the big upstairs bedrooms for himself, and brought in the blankets and cartons and luggage from the car. He went into the utility room and turned on the power-unit, remembering as he did so how his grandfather had disliked and distrusted the unit, how he had refused to have one until the electric wires were all gone and there was no other way to get power. He checked the stove and freezer, shoved his cartons of food into the latter, and looked around and wondered what to do next.

Standing in the silent house, he wondered suddenly if he had been foolish to quit everything and come back to Earth and this old place?

No, he thought heavily. Mercury ended it for me. I made my decision and that is that. Forget it.

He strode abruptly out of the house and started walking. And after a little while the dark weight in his mind, the somber knowledge, faded and receded in the newfound, old-remembered interest of the things about him.

His way took him across the road, past the shabby barns and up sloping pastures where once his grandfather had kept the fine horses he bred. Then he was in among the pines, climbing

# SCIENCE AND NATURE... STRANGE BEDFELLOWS

Here it is...our sixth collection of Science Fiction Gems. In it you will find a fantastic variety of wildly entertaining short stories, written by many of the best sci-fi writers of the twentieth century: Edmond Hamilton, Fritz Leiber, Murray Leinster, Jack Williamson, William Tenn and many others.

"Moons of Death" and "Tyrants Need to be Loved" are great examples of how the pendulum of blind devotion can swing easily from giving life...to taking it. "Travelling Companion Wanted" and "Death Sentence" offer two very interesting notions as to what may lay beyond our known and comfortable borders. And "Sunfire!," and "The Radio" show us that Mother Nature will almost always trump science.

Try out these sci-fi morsels in another collection of tales calculated to keep your mind pondering future possibilities.

# TABLE OF CONTENTS

# SCIENCE FICTION GEMS

## Volume 6

## EDMOND HAMILTON
### and others

**Compiled by Gregory Luce**

ARMCHAIR FICTION
PO Box 4369, Medford, Oregon 97504

*For more information about Armchair Books and products, visit our website at…*

**www.armchairfiction.com**

*Or email us at…*

**armchairfiction@yahoo.com**

more steeply, with the resinous smell of the trees strong in his nostrils. That smell he had never forgotten, and once he had met a smell vaguely like it, far away from Earth—

*Forget all that, Kellard.*

The trees took him in and he walked through a dapple of sun and shadows. A deer slipped away through the pines ahead of him, and quail burst up from almost under his feet. He remembered a grove of bigger pines farther up the slope, and an old man and a boy walking up to them. How long ago was that? He had been fifteen—and he was thirty-two now. Seventeen years. Still, he thought he could find the place.

He found it. The big pines were still there, for people did not use wood much any more. The rough dark giants stood at dignified intervals from each other, and he sat down with his back against the massive trunk of the biggest.

Funny, he thought. When I was a boy sitting here dreaming about the future and what I was going to do, I never once imagined that some things would stay much the same. The whole world would somehow be miraculously transformed—but it wasn't. This tree was here when men first reached the Moon, and Mars, and Venus and the rest, but it didn't know about that, it didn't change because of it.

KELLARD sat for a long time, still wrapped in a gray weariness, his emotions in a numb trance. He sat listening to the distant, uneasy murmur of the sea, until the sunset light shafting through the trees dazzled his eyes, and then he got up and went back down to the house. He heated food, ate it, and then went out to the porch in front of the house and sat watching the sun sink toward the vast golden sheet of the Pacific. He thought of the little dot close to the sun that he could not see, the little world and the strange, terrible place upon it where Morse and Binetti had died.

The telephone rang.

Kellard did not stir, and it rang and rang again.

Go ahead and ring your head off, he thought. You're not getting me back. I told you. I've had it.

The ringing stopped. The sun sank and darkness came with the hosts of wheeling stars, and there was no sound but the vast voices rolling in from sea, as Kellard sat staring and drinking. He finally got up, as the fog started coming in. He moved with gravity, feeling much better. He went in and turned on the lights, and then looked at the faces that stared from the long row of framed photographs.

He raised the bottle to them in a gesture of salutation.

"You see, Kellards, that your prodigal son—or great-grandson—has come home again from space."

He gravely drank, and continued to stand looking along the faded faces.

"You were lucky—you know that? Back in your time, there were hopes, and dreams, and man's road would go on forever, from triumph to triumph everlasting. But that road was a blind alley, all the time, even if I'm the only one who knows it."

The faces looked back at him, unchanging, but he read reproach in their steady gaze, their lined features.

"I'm sorry," said Kellard. "You had your own troubles, I know. I apologize, Kellards. I am very tired and a little drunk, and I am going to bed."

THE next morning he was making coffee when there came a banging of the old-fashioned knocker on the front door. A certain tightness came into Kellard's face. He had expected them to send someone.

He had not expected the man who stood at the door. He was not in Survey uniform, although he was the highest brass there was. He was a big, slow-moving man with a heavy face and blue eyes that seemed mild if you didn't know him.

"Well," said Kellard. And after a moment, "Come on in."

Halfrich came in. He sat down and looked interestedly around at the old room and furniture.

"Nice," he murmured. Then he looked at Kellard and said, "All right, let's have it. Why did you quit?"

Kellard shrugged. "It was all in my letter of resignation. I'm getting a bit old and tired for Survey, I—"

"Bull," said Halfrich. "It was something about that crack-up on Sunside, wasn't it?"

Kellard said slowly, "Yes. The deaths of Binetti and Morse, and the after-effects of that shock, made me feel I didn't have it any more."

Halfrich looked at him. "You've had crack-ups before. You've seen men die. You've had almost as many years in Survey as I have, and you've taken as many jolts. You're lying, Kellard."

Kellard got up, and walked a few steps and swung around again.

"So I'm lying. I want out, and what difference does it make why?"

"It makes a difference," Halfrich said grimly. "I remember from away back at Academy, even though you were two years after me. You were the space-craziest cadet there was. You spouted the glories of the conquest of space until we were all sick of it. You haven't changed in all the years in Survey—until now. I want to know what can change a man like that."

Kellard said nothing. He went to the window and looked out at the long rollers coming endlessly in and crashing against the rocks.

"What did you see on Sunside, Kellard?"

He turned around sharply at that.

"What do you mean? What would there be to see there, but hot rocks and volcanoes and a cross-section of hell generally? It's all in my report."

Halfrich sat like a judge, and spoke like one pronouncing sentence. "You saw something, you *met* something there. You covered by tearing out the film of the automatic sweep-camera. Whatever it had recorded, you didn't want us to see, did you?"

Kellard came toward him and spoke angrily and rapidly. "Do you realize that we flamed out and crashed there? A crash like that can do damage. It killed Binetti and mortally injured Morse, and smashed the sweep-camera."

Halfrich nodded. "That's what we thought, at first. But the radar-sweep had an automatic recorder too. It was something new. Binetti knew about it, as communications officer, but I guess he hadn't told you, or you'd have smashed it, too. Its record shows something."

A COLD feeling came over Kellard. He had thought that he had covered every thing, but he had calculated from insufficient data.

He kept his nerve. A radar record was not like a photograph, they couldn't prove much from that, they certainly couldn't guess the truth from it. They *must* not guess the truth.

He laughed mirthlessly. "A radar record made on Sunside isn't worth the paper it's on. The storms of radiation there make radar practically unreliable."

Halfrich was watching him keenly. "But not entirely. And over and above the static and the fake bogies, the record shows quite clearly that you went outside the ship after the crash, that you walked about a thousand yards, and that you were approached by some things that register vaguely but unmistakably."

He paused and then he asked, "Who—or what—did you meet there, Kellard?"

Kellard was cold inside, but all the same he made a disgusted sound that he hoped was convincing.

"Who would I meet on Sunside? Beautiful lightly clad maidens? After all, you know, it's only four hundred degrees centigrade there, and practically no atmosphere, and nothing much else but solar radiation and hot rock and volcanoes. I tell you, the radar record is worthless."

Halfrich was studying him with that mild estimating look that Kellard knew well, and didn't like at all. It was the look that came into Halfrich's face when friendship didn't matter and the good of the Survey did.

"You're still lying," he said. "You met or saw something there. And it did something to you—something that made you resign. Something that's taken all the life and eagerness out of you."

"Oh, hell, be reasonable," said Kellard angrily. "You know no kind of life can exist on Sunside. My mission was the second time ever Survey has landed there. Pavlik's mission, the first, didn't see anything. Neither did I. Quit dreaming it up. Go back to Mojave and your job, and leave me be."

HALFRICH rose. "All right," he said. "I'll go back to the base. And you're going with me."

"Oh, no," said Kellard. "I'm through, quit, resigned."

"Your resignation has not been accepted," Halfrich told him. "You're still liable to Survey discipline. You'll obey orders just as you always did, or you'll go up before a court-martial."

"So that's it," said Kellard.

Halfrich nodded. "That is it. I don't like to do this. You're an old friend. But—"

"But the Survey comes first," Kellard said, between his teeth.

"The Survey," said Halfrich, "comes first. It has to. It's why we've got stations on Venus and Mars and Ganymede, not to say the Moon. It's why we'll someday be able to hit for deep space and the starworlds. And when one of my best officers suddenly goes off the deep end and won't say why, I'll damn well wring it out of him. Whatever you found on Mercury doesn't belong to you, it belongs to us, and we'll have it."

Kellard looked at him and started to say something and didn't, and then turned his back on Halfrich and looked out the window at the sea. In a low voice he said,

"Let it be, John. I'm telling you now, you'll be sorry if you don't."

There was no answer to that at all, and the silence was his answer. He turned back around.

"All right, you have a rope around my neck. I'll go back to base with you. I'll tell you not one thing more than here."

"In which case," Halfrich said, "we'll go on out to Sunside, and you'll go right along with us."

A rage born of desperation came to Kellard. He had tried to spare people this—Halfrich, the Survey, the whole human race. But they would not let it be so. Damn them, he thought, if they must do this, they have it coming to them.

"All right," he said flatly. "I'll get my jacket. I take it that you have a flier waiting."

THE fast flier, less than an hour later, whizzed down over the gaunt mountains and across the desert, and the glitter and splendor of Mojave Base sprang up to meet them. The tall ships shone like silver, and something about them, something about the feel of the place, made you think that this bit of desert did not belong to Earth at all but was part of space, a way-station, the first way-station of all, to the stars.

That, thought Kellard, was what he had thought when he had first come here, years ago. And it had not been just a youngster's passing enthusiasm, it had deepened and strengthened through all the years of work and danger—until Sunside. And oh God, he thought, why did I have to go there, at that place, at that moment. I could have lived my whole life and done my work, all of us could have, without ever dreaming the truth.

He knew now that he had no choice. He must go back to Sunside with them. For even if he told them the truth, they would not believe, they would insist on going to see for themselves. He would keep silent, and that was all he could do now.

\*　\*　\*

Four days later a Y-90 experimental cruiser, outfitted for space research and with full anti-heater equipment, took off from Mojave. Kellard had kept silent. And still silent he sat in his recoil-harness and took the jolts, and heard Halfrich grunting beside him, and viciously hoped that that he was not liking it.

Halfrich had brought along a consulting biophysicist, a keen-faced man of middle age named Morgenson, who did not look as though he was enjoying the mission either. But the three-man crew of the little Y-90 were young men in their twenties. They spoke to Halfrich and to Kellard as though they were heroes out of legend, for in the Survey twelve to fifteen years of space missions was an age.

It was only after they had gone a long way and a long time through the sun-washed spaces that one of the three, Shay, the navigator, ventured to put a question to Kellard.

"You were with the first mission to Ganymede, sir, weren't you?"

Kellard nodded. "Yes, I was."

"Wouldn't that have been something," said Shay. "I mean, to be the first."

"It was something," said Kellard.

"Maybe someday I—" Shay began, and broke off and then went on, "I mean, if the star-drive is perfected as soon as some people say it will be, I could maybe be one of the first ones out there? Sir?"

"You could be," said Kellard. "Someone's going to be first. The stars are waiting. All we have to do is go out there and keep going, and the stars will be ours, just like the planets here are all ours, forever and amen."

Shay looked at him puzzledly, and shuffled, and then went away. Halfrich had been listening, and watching. He said, "Did you have to slap the kid's face?"

Kellard shrugged. "What did I say? I was merely repeating what everyone feels these days. The glory of the conquest of space."

"I'd give a lot," Halfrich said, "to know what's riding you. We'll soon reach Sunside and we'll find out, but I wish you'd tell me now."

"All right," said Kellard. "I'll tell you, I've been disinherited. That's what's wrong with me."

HE would say nothing more, nor did Halfrich ask him another question, until the Y-90 was far in past the orbit of Venus and going into its pattern of approach.

"I assume," said Halfrich, "that you bear none of us any personal ill-will. If there is anything dangerous awaiting us, now would be the time to tell us."

Kellard considered. "You're going to land, I suppose, at the same spot where we crashed."

"Of course."

"Then land, said Kellard. "As far as I know, there is not a thing there to harm you."

In the scanner, he watched Mercury swing slowly toward them, a tiny crescent of white that was hard to see against the Sun. For here the Sun was a monster thing, fringed with writhing flames, paling the stars, drenching this whole area with radiation that already would have killed them but for the ship's anti-heaters.

Kellard remembered that when he had come this way before, Binetti had quoted something, a line from William Blake's poems, he had said. *"The desire of the moth for the star."* And that was what we were, he thought. Three little moths, going right into the furnace, and I was the only one to get out of it, but now I'm going back.

The Y-90 went into its landing pattern. It skimmed over the dark side of Mercury, the black cliffs and peaks and chasms that never saw the Sun, and then light seemed to burst ragingly up from all the horizon ahead of them, and they were over Sunside.

In old days this little world had been called "the moon of the Sun," and it looked like it, the same stark, lifeless rock plains and ridges and cracks, the fang-like look of pinnacles in a place where no atmosphere eroded anything. But the Moon was cold and still, whereas Sunside seemed to throb with sullen hidden fires. Volcanoes spewed ash and lava, and the infernal storm of radiation from overhead made everything quiver in a shimmering haze. The indicator board told them that the temperature of the outside hull was climbing to four hundred as the Y-90 went down.

And the wide valley that haunted his dreams opened up ahead.

Across it the squat volcanic cones still dribbled ash and dust and it was all just as it had been when he had last looked back from the relief cruiser that had come from Venus Station to take him off. And there gleamed bright on its floor the crumpled wreck in which Binetti and then Morse had died.

Kellard's gaze flew to the place north of the wreck, the tumbled, odd-shaped rocks. He felt his palms sweating. Maybe there would be nothing. After all, could it all happen again?

They set down, and after the crashing rocket uproar, the steady throb of the anti-heaters was an anti-climactic sound.

"You've got the armor ready?" Halfrich asked of Morgenson.

The biophysicist nodded nervously. "Three suits with their anti-heater equipment tested on and off all the way out."

"One suit stays here, for emergencies," Halfrich said. "Kellard and I will go out, when there's something to go out for. First, we'll make observations."

THE recording telescope-cameras and the radar, Halfrich ordered focused on the place of the odd-shaped rocks. And then, sitting there on Sunside, they watched. They waited.

Nothing.

Kellard's hopes began to rise. He was right, he told himself, it couldn't happen again.

"How long," he asked, "are we going to sit waiting for nothing because a radar made a screwy record? If those antiheaters quit for five minutes, we're fried."

Halfrich looked at him bleakly. "I'll tell you how long. Till you tell the truth, and we see the truth for ourselves. That's how long."

Kellard shrugged. "If that's the way you want it. I would tell you to go to hell except that we're already there."

They watched and waited some more.

Morgenson said, on a rising note of excitement, "There's something—"

Halfrich got to the scope fast. Kellard, looking through the scanner, saw the geyser of flame that was beginning to pour up from the rocks. It grew slowly, but steadily, in height.

"What is it?" Halfrich asked him.

"Can't you see for yourself?" said Kellard. "There's a blowhole out there and it throws off burning gases from the interior. It did it twice while I was waiting in the wreck."

Halfrich said, "It's in the same location where radar recorded you before, with those other blips. There's something about this— We'll go have a look."

"If you must," said Kellard. "You'll find it's just what I've said."

They got into the heat-armor. It was a clumsy outfit, for it had to have room for an efficient anti-heater, and the long tube of the heat-discharge was a nuisance. Kellard had spent days in one of these suits, waiting for the relief ship after the crack-up, and he did not like the feel of it at all.

Halfrich tested the radio and then said, "All right, Shay, lock us out and stand by. Morgenson, you keep watching."

They stepped upon Sunside.

There beat down upon them such a storm of radiation, such cataracts of heat and light, that instinctively they bowed their heads as before a deluge. It took an effort of will to step forward through that tempest, but Halfrich made it. They walked, slowly and heavily, and at first they saw only the blackened rocks beneath their feet, and the little puddles and rivulets of molten lead, and their own massive armored feet plodding.

Then, as they went forward, they straightened against the impact. Through the faceplate of his armor, dimmed by the many-layered filters, Kellard saw the column of flame ahead. It was a hundred feet high now, and growing higher, and though there was no airborne sound on this almost airless world, the sound of it came through the rocks and the soles of their feet, a throbbing and roaring that quivered through all their bodies.

THEY reached the tumbled rocks, and stopped. And now the fire-fountain was so lofty that they had to lean back their heads to look at its topmost crest. Some unthinkable diastole and systole of the fiery planet was at work, and this periodic geyser of flame was its result. The rocks shook and roared, and the fires raged higher, and Kellard thought again, what devil is in the blood of our race that drives us to places like this where we should not be?

"I told you," he said to Halfrich. "Just a blowhole, that's all."

"The blips on the record moved," said Halfrich. "There was more than this."

"Look around you!" cried Kellard desperately. "Do you see anything moving, anything that *could* move? You were wrong, Halfrich. Do you have to keep us here until we all die, because you can't admit you're wrong?"

Halfrich hesitated. "I wasn't wrong. You're still lying. But we'll go back to the ship and wait."

They turned their backs on the fire-fountain, and Kellard felt the sweat pouring on his forehead. It hadn't happened this time, and they couldn't wait forever, they would have to go away and—

Morgenson's voice chattered in their ears. "Blips showing, coming—" And then he suddenly yelled, "I see them! They—"

Halfrich swung around with ponderous swiftness. There was nothing between them and the fire-fountain, nothing around the spouting flames.

"Above you, coming down!" shouted Morgenson. "My God, what—?"

Kellard slowly raised his head. Because he knew what to look for, he saw them while Halfrich was still gazing around searching.

They came flashing down out of the sky. There were four of them this time—no, five. They were like five individual swirls of shining light, so bright that the sun-bleached heavens seemed to darken around them.

Halfrich said bewilderedly, "I don't see—"

Kellard pointed upward. "There."

"Those flakes of flame?"

"Not flakes of flame," said Kellard. "They are the children of the stars."

Halfrich went rigid, staring upward. And now Kellard knew that there was no more hope. No hope at all.

THE five bright things had flashed down toward the great fire-fountain. They plunged into it, out of it, climbed swift as the eye could follow, racing up its mighty geyser, frolicking in it joyously. The fountain raved higher and the five sped up and whirled and danced upon its rising plume, and Kellard thought that they were laughing.

In and out of the leaping fires they plunged, and then one of them veered down toward the place where Halfrich and Kellard stood. There was something so humanly purposeful in its sudden movement that Halfrich stepped back.

"Stand still," said Kellard.

"But—" Halfrich protested.

"They won't hurt us," said Kellard, his voice flat and dull. "They're friendly, playful, curious. Stand still."

And now all five of the flashing flames were around them, darting, recoiling, then gliding forward again to touch their heat-armor with questing tendrils of living force, living light.

Halfrich spoke, trying to keep his voice steady but forming the words in a choked fashion.

"Something—in my mind—"

"They're telepathic, in a way you can't even imagine," said Kellard. "And they're curious. They're curious, about us, what we are, how we think. They can merge minds with us, somehow." And he added, with a last cruel impulse of dying anger, "You wanted to know. Now know."

He had time to say nothing more before the impact hit him, just as it had that other time, the full stunning shock of unearthly minds interlocking with his own, searching out his thoughts and memories.

Curious, yes. Like children who have found strange, ungainly creatures and wish to know how they live. And as they entered his mind, Kellard's mind entered theirs, fused with them, and there was again the dizzying whirl of memories and feelings that were not his own—that his different, more brutishly physical nature could never apprehend more than dimly.

But that half-apprehension was staggering. He was no longer Hugh Kellard, a man with flesh and bones who had been born on an air-drowned heavy planet named Earth.

He was one of the children of the stars.

His memory stretched far back, for his life was almost unlimited in time. For long and long beyond human comprehension he had lived with his companions the strange and beautiful life of their kind.

Born of the stars, of the unimaginable forces, pressures, temperatures, atomic conditions within the mighty suns. Born, as the end product of an evolutionary chain almost as old as the universe itself, a grouping of photons that grew toward consciousness, toward individuality and volition. Their bodies were force, rather than matter, their senses had nothing to do with sight or hearing, their movement was an effortless flash and glide as fast as the photons of light itself.

WITH the other kind of life in the universe, the heavy slow-moving things of matter that grew upon the comparatively cold, dark planets, they had had nothing to do at all. They were of the suns, not the planets, and those chill worlds of fixed, solid matter so repelled them that they would not even approach most of them.

Star-child, star-child, at home in the bursting splendors of the stellar fires, and able to move like light from star to star. And again Kellard felt the agony of that ecstasy that was his in this shared memory.

*"We things of matter, we men, who thought that space and the stars would be ours——"*

But how could the wide universe belong to solid, heavy, physical creatures who must painfully move in bubbles of air, who crawled between the petty planets encased in metal tombs, who could not even approach the glories of the great suns?

No, the ecstasy was one that men would never know except at secondhand through this brief contact. The glorious rush together of the star-children through the vast abysses, drinking up the energy of the radiation about them. The audacious and dangerous coasting along the shores of dark nebulae, racing the lumbering comets and leaving them behind, on until you felt through all your photons the beckoning warmth of the star you approached. Ignore the cinders called planets that creep around it, speed faster, faster, brothers, the way has been long but we are almost there! And now the radiation that was so weak in the outer darks is strong and lusty-roaring, and the great prominences reach out like arms to gather us in. The shock, the joy, of the first plunge once more into the star. Dive deep, brothers, deep through the outer fires into the throbbing solar furnaces where the atoms are hammered as in forges, changing, shifting their shapes, exploding into force.

Spin in the vortices of the great stellar tornadoes, fling off and fall headlong and then dive laughing in again. Search for the others of your kind, if there are none here there will be at the next star. Up again, out of the boiling fires, and then drift quiet, dreaming, in the pearly glow of the corona, endless afternoon of warmth and light and peace.

BUT on the sunward side of the tiny planet nearby, a plaything beckons. Fire and light fountain up from the solid rock. There at least we can go, for that place is washed by tides of solar life, not chilled and dead. Speed down toward it, as the fire, the life it spouts higher out of the repellently fixed and solid matter. Frolic in the fountain, through and around it as it rises higher. And what are the things that move on the rock near it, the things that look grotesquely as though matter had been endowed with life? Reach out with your thought-senses and try to apprehend them. Mind, life-in matter! Try to understand how matter thinks, how matter feels, plumb the grotesque memories of them, the vistas of crawling things at the bottom of whelming air-oceans, things of clay too frail to endure, yet things that in their brief living have come here. But the mind recoils from such memories, such a life.

Brothers, we go! First to refresh ourselves in the deepest streams of the star, and then away across the abysses to another star we know. There is nothing to hold us here—

And the oneness was gone from Kellard's mind, and he was no child of light and stars, he was a man of clay, standing stupid and sick and shaking by the falling fires of the fountain.

He looked at Halfrich. But Halfrich stood, with his head bowed, and Kellard felt only pity.

He touched his arm. "We'll go back to the ship."

For a long moment, Halfrich did not respond. Then he turned and walked, plodding with head down, not looking up once at the flaring sky.

\* \* \*

In the little ship, he sat later with Kellard. He had not spoken yet, and Morgenson and the others, bewildered and awed, had still not dared ask questions. Finally Halfrich looked at Kellard, pain still in his eyes.

"I was thinking," he said. "I was remembering my little boy, years ago. He had just learned to walk, and he started out the door, eager to explore the whole town. He stubbed his toe, and he sat down and cried."

"You tried to spare me this," said Halfrich after a little while. "Thanks for that, Kellard. It didn't work, but thanks anyway."

Kellard said, "Look, no one else knows. No one else is ever likely to know. The only place where the men of matter and the children of stars could meet is a place like Sunside, and how many such meetings would ever by chance happen? We don't have to tell everyone, to take the heart and eagerness out of them by letting them know they'll always be second-best in space."

Halfrich thought about that. And then he shook his head. "No. We've stubbed our toe. We've learned we're not and never will be the sole inheritors of the universe. O.K., we'll accept the fact and go on. The planets will be ours, just the same. And someday—" He paused, then said, "—someday, maybe, the sons of the planets and the children of stars will take hands, know each other. No, Kellard. We'll tell them."

## THE END

# My Brother's Keeper

## By ALFRED COPPEL

*He found himself being torn between two loves: one could bring him complete happiness; the other only a monument...*

GREG ELY walked down the street from the Bureau filled with a sick despair. It was early March and an icy wind was blowing, driving grit and rubble before it through the nearly deserted canyons of the city. There were a few workers left on the streets, but these were hurrying home to beat the dusk curfew, their collars turned up against the cold. The city was bleak and cheerless, and Greg let himself think of Elna. Right now he wanted only to be with her—to let her comfort him. He wanted to seek her out and try to explain his failure. But that was what he must not do. It was bad enough that he had let himself be trapped. He dare not lead the Monitors to Elna and the others.

Ely forced himself to walk slowly. It was a better than even chance that he was being followed now. The back of his neck tingled with anticipation of an electro-bolt that might lash out from any dark doorway. The Monitors worked that way sometimes. Then the Party newssheet would carry a brief paragraph in the morning about the mysterious death of an obscure rocket man—and a mock search for nonexistent saboteurs would rout a dozen or so workers out of their warrens and pack them off to the Camps. The murder of an "unreliable" would make no great uproar in a city that lived with death.

The narco examination had been routine. Every worker assigned to the Mars Project took one twice a year. But something had gone wrong. Marsden's mnemonic blocks had failed. They must have failed. The Director had been evasive—too evasive. And he was free, for the time being, at least. The Monitors did nothing without reason. So the only answer was that he was bait. Small fry. They could afford to turn him loose in the hope that he would run for the others.

Greg moved slowly between the rows of grey, soot-stained buildings. This, he thought bleakly, was what failure felt like. For three years he had worked in the Mars Project. The Underground felt it important to have someone in the planned colony on Mars. But the watchdogs of the People's State had sniffed him out. The dream was finished.

The murky grey of the sky was deepening into dismal blackness as Greg reached the Square. The curfew hour had passed now and the streets were devoid to life. No citizen was allowed out after dark within the city. It was one of the trifling sacrifices, Greg thought drily, that the people made for the New Democracy.

ORDINARILY, Greg Ely would have been in his own smelly tenement room by this time, but his discharge from the Mars Project and his hopelessness was tempting him to petty defiances.

The Square was an analogy of the State, Greg thought as he looked out over the vast expanse of asphalt. The pillboxes around the perimeter—covered with bright posters redundant with promises of plenty in some future date—did not quite hide the blunt muzzles of the electro-blasters within. It was here that the people paraded under the threat of instant death. The vastness of the Square was symbolic of the world-wide dominion of the State. And then the final irony. The Monument. An obelisk of black stone a hundred meters high, and atop this the huge figure of the Common Man, a monster spanner in his hand, and his blunt features raised toward the stars...

Greg stared at the mammoth figure. There was something in the yearning pose that struck a spark. An idea began to form. A defiant, impossible idea. The human mind is strange, Greg thought. Offer it freedom and then snatch it away and the mind begins to search. Eventually a plan takes shape. Even a wild, impossible sort of plan—but a *plan*.

The wind ripped away long strips of the cloudy sky and the looming colossus was etched in blackness against the faint stars. From across the Square came the faint wail of a siren. It was far away. The three headlamps of a gyrocar appeared and began to move swiftly across the asphalt toward Greg Ely. For a moment he connected the siren with the approaching car, but as the car drew near he realized that this was not so. The car approached in silence, and as it did so, its lights went dark.

Without quite knowing why, Greg began to run. Now that he had a plan there was a reason to keep fighting. He ran for the cover of a narrow alleyway, his breath coming hard and his pulse pounding.

He heard someone call to him from the dark gyrocar, but he did not slow down. Escape was the only important thing now. He had a plan to substitute for his failure. He had something to offer Marsden and the others. Something to offer Elna…

He was still running when a low-power electro-bolt caught him and sent him sprawling in the street. Paralysis held him rigid as the dark gyrocar slowed—stopped. He felt many hands pulling him into the vehicle.

He heard someone say: "Hurry! The Monitors are coming!" Then he felt the silken acceleration of the car under him and heard the keening of the siren in the distance.

A protecting darkness folded itself about him as his synapses failed under the shock of the electro. Very slowly, he tumbled into a velvet abyss shot with fiery streaks…

HE AWOKE in a dingy room that might have been his own, but it wasn't. His head throbbed painfully from the after-effects of the electro-bolt and his limbs felt leaden.

He lay in a tenement somewhere. That much was certain. The smell of cooking food clung to the very walls and the faded threadbare bedclothes that covered him smelled of insect-powder.

The door opened and a girl entered. Ely felt his heart skip. It was Elna. His friends had picked him up—and the Monitors must have seen.

"I was so afraid for you, Greg," Elna said. "They had to hurt you to bring you here. Why did you run?"

Greg managed a wan smile. "I ran, that's all. Maybe I thought it was the Monitors."

Elna stood uncertainly beside him. In the dim light one could not see the lines of fatigue that marred her face, or the streaks of premature grey in her hair. Even the short singlet of rough denim that reached halfway down her thighs—the garb of a factory worker—became her. Her feet and legs were bare. Thin, too, Greg noticed with a pang. There was never quite enough food for the workers, and none could afford shoes except in the coldest part of the winter.

"Elna…" He sat up with an effort and caught her by the hand, pulling her to him. Suddenly his plan seemed more important than before. He held her tightly, feeling her gaunt, work-hardened body against his. Freedom for Elna was more important than freedom for himself. He was almost glad the primary plan had failed.

Presently Marsden came in and Greg released Elna reluctantly.

"I see you've recovered," Marsden said drily.

"We can't stay here, Marsden," Greg said. "Monitors were following me when you picked me up."

"I know."

"How long have we?"

"Ten minutes, perhaps. Maybe more."

"Have they picked anybody up?"

"Moulder and Warnecke."

"Then I talked," exclaimed Ely bitterly.

"They gave you a narco?" Marsden asked.

"Yes. I must have babbled plenty. The mnemonic blocks didn't work. Why?"

Marsden shrugged. "That happens sometimes. You can build up only so much resistance to narco synthesis. When your limit of tolerance is reached—you talk."

"Could they have implanted a posthypnotic suggestion?"

"It's possible, though not likely. Why?"

For a moment Ely thought in silence. It was not beyond the realm of possibility that his plan was the product of a Monitor psych's brain. But he had talked under the narco. They had to chance it. He knew all the important members of the Underground—and now he had let himself be rescued. Therefore the Monitors couldn't be far off. It was act now—or die.

"They'll have all of us by tomorrow, you know," he said, trying to keep his voice steady. "Why did you pick me up?"

MARSDEN smiled bleakly. "We had to take the chance. You're the only rocket expert we have." He shrugged. "At that we almost had to kill you. Everything's fouled up now. You being in the Mars Project was our last hope. There was nowhere else to turn. So—" He broke off abruptly, his eyes hard. "We can use the arms cache to make a stand in the storm drains. It won't prove anything, but at least we can take some of those swine to perdition with us."

"Then everyone is resigned to making a fight of it?"

"Yes. What else is there left to do?"

"All right," Ely said. "That fits in. I have a plan. As long as there's no other way out, we may as well make the fight count for something."

"Meaning what?" asked Marsden.

"Meaning we try to steal the rocket."

*"What?"*

"It makes sense, Marsden. Listen. The Project Bureau has spent ten years building the spaceship for the try at Mars. That means another couldn't possibly be built in less than three years. They've set the launching date for next week—you didn't know that?"

"No."

"It has to be within a week either way of March 30. Tomorrow is the first day. And get this: *oppositions of Mars come only every fifteen years.*"

*"Fifteen years!"*

"Have you any idea what the possibilities are? Think, man! The rocket is intended to set up a colony. That means it is fully provisioned and equipped. If we can get off tomorrow in it, we're *free!* There can be no pursuit for at least three years and most likely for *fifteen!*"

Marsden stared. His mind filled suddenly with a new vision of freedom. An Underground colony on Mars. It would have time to establish itself, time to plan a defense against the assault that would surely come from Earth and the People's State.

"But—even if we could pull this off," he protested, "what about pilotage? What about landing? There are a million problems."

"Don't split hairs, Marsden! I can handle the rocket controls. The landing is planned to be by parachute. It's been tested. It works, even in thin air. The rest of it can be worked out as problems arise. The important thing is getting the spaceship. And it will have to be tomorrow." He managed a bleak grin. "After all, Comrade, it is worth the try, don't you think?"

Marsden laid a hand on Greg's shoulder. "You say *you* will handle the rocket controls?"

"Yes." He searched Marsden's features. The older man's face was set. *Marsden knew.* Greg hurried on, throwing words into the breach. "Think what it will mean, Marsden. A colony of free men on a free world..."

Marsden looked at Elna. Greg wondered how much the girl knew. Nothing about the rocket, thank God. And Marsden wouldn't tell her.

"All right, Greg," Marsden said in a low voice. "I'll tell the others."

"Transportation?" Greg wanted to get the conversation away from the spaceship now. It was important that only he and Marsden know the joker in his plan.

"I'll attend to it."

"Tomorrow, then."

Marsden turned and started to leave. At the door, he turned abruptly, and Greg had the feeling that he was going to spill everything to Elna. He opened his mouth to speak— but the sudden shrieking of a siren cut him off.

*"Monitors!"* Elna said.

"Stay together, you two," Marsden said, and then he gave a short, hard laugh that cut into Greg like a knife.

"Head for the storm drains. Meet us tomorrow at the weapons cache. I'll have cars there to take us all to the rocket base." Marsden looked again at Greg. "Good luck," he said, and was gone.

GREG PULLED himself painfully from the cot and donned his jumper. Then together, he and the girl slipped out into the grimy hallway. They had reached the stairway when the first gyrocar of Monitors arrived. Searchlights splashed the facade of the old building. The metallic voice of a public address system began warning the inhabitants to stay in their rooms. Cordons were being set up around the block.

Elna and Greg reached the street level and emerged out of a side entrance into a narrow, littered alleyway between buildings. She led the way to the blind end or the alley and began digging in the refuse. Greg lent his strength to the task, and soon a small manhole cover lay bare. He lifted it and stared for a moment into the stygian darkness of the pit.

They squeezed through and into the darkness. Greg replaced the cover and dropped to the damp concrete floor. The drain smelled wet and old, and from somewhere in the distance there came the sound of running water.

Elna slipped her hand into his and they moved forward, down the sloping tunnel. Greg produced a small torch from his jumper pocket and they moved along in a sphere of dim radiance.

New tubes joined theirs at intervals, and at each, Elna paused to inspect the numbers imbedded in the concrete. For what seemed hours, they walked along, through dark icy water that reached in some places to their waists.

At last they reached a rising side-tunnel that branched out of theirs. Elna inspected the numbers with care and led the way upward. Perhaps a hundred meters from the junction a caved in section blocked further progress. Here the girl stopped. A pile of blankets and a small cache of canned food lay in the corner. Greg sank wearily down onto the curving concrete. His head still ached from the after-effects of the electro-bolt and he was chilled to the bone.

Elna opened a can of food and they sat and ate in silence. They stripped off their wet clothes and wrapped up in blankets. Greg felt suddenly very tired. He lay back and wearily closed his eyes.

He must have slept for a short time, for when he opened his eyes again, the light was out and Elna lay at his side. He reached out and touched her. Her hair was coarse and dry under his hands, her flesh rough. She sighed contentedly and moved closer to him, whispering faintly in her sleep. Greg felt a tightness in his throat. She was a simple creature. She wanted only freedom—and Greg. As simple as that. But nothing came without a price tag. Ely closed his eyes and tried to force the bleak thoughts out of his mind.

Greg stretched out and let his tired muscles relax. Presently he slept, and he dreamed of low red hills under a cobalt sky. Greg Ely dreamed of Mars...

NIGHT WAS falling as Ely and Marsden topped the ridge that faced the guarded launching site. The others of the Underground were behind them, a pitifully small group of armed men and women spaced out among the scrubby bushes that grew on the slopes. They had come out of the city by gyrocar, twenty men and fifteen women. Now, with pounding heart, Greg was leading them forward toward the rocket field.

The weight of the automatic rifle was unfamiliar on his back, and his head still ached painfully, but Greg felt a savage excitement quicken the blood in his veins.

The field was flood-lighted and Marsden and Greg could see the spaceship clearly. Some quirk of memory likened the slender projectile to the Monument in Greg's mind. Both seeking the freedom of the stars—but only one destined to have the chance.

The field was guarded by spaced gun-towers and a fence of charged wire. Electro-blasts were mounted in the towers, and much of Greg's plan of assault depended on them. His eyes narrowed as he saw the open door to the Central

Control pillbox. A green-clad Monitor was lolling there, smoking carelessly.

"You take the main body and wait under cover near the main gate," Greg told Marsden. "Give me two grenades. When you hear one let go up here, rush the gates. The current in the fence will be dead. Rush the ship. Never mind anything else. Get everyone in the ship and close the valves. I'll take care of the rest." He saw that Marsden was about to protest and he cut him off curtly. "This is important, Marsden. Remember, I'm willing to do my part. You should be willing to do yours."

"All right," Marsden said. "I'll send the grenades up." He turned away and inched his way back to where the rest of the rebels waited. Shortly, Greg saw Elna crawling up the slope with the grenades. She wore an electro-blast around her waist, and her face had been blackened with soot.

"The grenades, Greg," she whispered. "Will they be enough?"

"Plenty. Did Marsden pass the rest around?"

The girl nodded.

"Good. Now—" He hesitated. This was the hard part of it. "You go back with the others," he said.

"I want to go with you," she replied simply.

"Please. Go back, Elna." He looked long into her face, memorizing every feature. This would have to last a long time. He looked away quickly. Perhaps not so long at that. "Go on now, Elna. We'll have time together later." The words almost stuck in his throat.

"A lifetime," she said softly. She kissed him, smudging his face with soot. Then she was gone. He closed his eyes tightly, not wanting to see her go. When he opened them again there was nothing but the silent slopes and the silvery shape of the spaceship.

Greg inched his way down the slope toward the charged fence. He reached the cleared area before being discovered, and then, as the searchlight found him, he broke into a run for the charged wire. Just short of it he stopped, unslinging his rifle and loosing a barrage of slugs at the watchtower.

His plan worked. Under attack, the Monitors acted rashly. They swung the electro-blast around. Greg cringed inwardly, but he held his ground. The wire fence was between him and the belled muzzle. He watched the nimbus of fire form and leap toward him. He could not help closing his eyes, but the bolt struck the charged fence and shorted. A half-million volts surged into the wire and it glowed cherry-red. There was a flash and the stench of ozone and the wire melted. The fence was down.

GREG LEAPED forward and pulled the pin from a grenade. It arced toward the watchtower and exploded into a blossom of fire. The watchtower collapsed in a rain of debris.

An answering blast from down the line told him that Marsden was beginning his attack. He began to run toward the launching ramp. A gyrocar cut out of the confusion of the base and came sweeping toward him. He met it with a fusillade of armor-piercing slugs from his rifle and it tumbled as the projectiles shattered the flywheel. Greg had a fleeting glimpse of white, agonized faces within as the shards of the gyro slashed through the car's occupants.

Suddenly the field went dark. Either the Monitors had cut off the power to confuse the attackers or Marsden had blasted the generating station. That was bad. Power was needed to launch the rocket.

Tracers and electro-bolts lit the darkness. A siren began a belated wailing. Shots crackled all along the line as the surprised Monitors raked the surrounding hills with their deadly fire.

Greg ran toward the ramp, his last grenade in his hand, the heavy rifle thumping on his back. He was almost there when the emergency power came on and lights etched the confusion against the pressing night.

Overhead a jetplane roared. The Monitors had already called for help from the city. There was little time left. Greg gave a shout of triumph as he saw that Marsden, under cover of the brief darkness, had succeeded in getting the rebels aboard the spaceship. The last of them was filing into the valve high up amid the maze of scaffolding.

A searing blast caught the end of the queue and cooked it. Greg looked around to see a light field-projector leveling for another shot. He pulled the pin from his last grenade and threw it. The blaster and its crew erupted in a ball of greasy flame. The valve on the spaceship's flank closed.

Now there was one thing left to do, and it was up to Greg alone. He ran for the pillbox, his rifle spitting steel, raking the nearby buildings.

A burly Monitor guessed his intention and moved in to block him. Greg cut him down with a burst. He was nearly to the pillbox now; two more Monitors started toward him. He sprayed them with slugs until the gun went silent. Empty.

An air bomb exploded near the spaceship with an earth-shaking roar. Greg felt his heart sink. The Monitors were willing to destroy the ship itself rather than let it be stolen.

Greg dived for the pillbox just as a blast from some unseen rifle caught him in the small of the back and spun him around. Pain almost blinded him. He staggered erect and into the concrete box. He slammed the steel door shut and turned toward the banks of switches. His jumper was soaked with blood and he felt darkness plucking at him. He had to stay on his feet at all costs!

A sullen roar began under the rocket. Flickers of flame splashed against the ramp, eating away the flimsy scaffolding.

A bomb fell nearby and the control room rocked, the steel door sagging on its hinges.

The fire grew brighter. The spaceship stirred, lifted. Greg could feel the vibrations and the heat of the tail-blast. The radarscope brightened. The spaceship was well up now, rising through a lattice of tracer-fire with agonizing slowness. Greg punched keys on the computers rapidly, fighting his failing strength. At last it was done, the course set.

He turned on the intercom and called Marsden. Without waiting for a reply he gave instructions. Marsden acknowledged, nothing more. Greg began to laugh. He was thinking of Mars again. Of the low red hills he had seen so often in dreams. Of the cobalt sky where the stars shone night and day—

"Greg! Greg!" Elna's voice came through the intercom, but faintly. "Greg! Where are you?"

He did not answer. In his mind he could see those ancient hills. Elna was there, walking under the cloudless sky. She was free: he didn't want to spoil it. He didn't want to say that he had lied to her—that he never intended to go with her, that the spaceship was remotely controlled and that she had to pay for her freedom with his life. Greg closed his eyes and his head sank toward his chest. Dark shadows flickered before his eyes, but they did not dim the vision of Mars.

Elna's voice was very, very faint now. He reached out gropingly and snapped off the instrument. The Monitors were battering down the door. He didn't want Elna to hear what came next. He smiled and sank back into his dream. The crash of the door was unheard, the rattling fusillade that cut him down at the panel was unfelt.

Far above him, the spaceship reached for the stars.

## THE END

# Moons Of Death

## By DAVID V. REED

*Hanley was the best "moon-diver" in the business, but someone was out
to "get" him. He didn't know who until he found himself diving blind,
compass wrecked, and a liner's fate depending on guesswork.*

OLD Rugger Hanley said evenly, "I'm not drunk, Kieller,
and you know it. Now give me those lenses and let me go to
work."

Samuel Kieller, general manager of the Ceres Company,
smiled. "I think you've had a little too much of that Martian
*behla,* Rugger. I was watching you as you came across the
field. You could hardly walk erect."

"It's nothing," said Hanley quietly. He rubbed a hand
across his lined, weather-beaten face, brushed back his
greying hair. "It's just that after Tom Worth crashed on the
moons..." His voice died away. "You don't think I'd take
any chances up there, do you, Kieller?"

"I'm not worried about you, Rugger. A moon-diver is one
life, but when he's piloting in a space liner, hundreds of lives
are in his hands. Remember that. Here are your glasses."
Kieller opened the huge wall safe and took out a large pair of
dark glasses. Stamped into the glass itself was the
Interplanetary Patrol seal, Hanley's full name and his
resignation number. Those special Haydite lenses were the
key to Corellan commerce; they had to be carefully guarded.

Rugger Hanley took the proffered glasses, turned, and
walked slowly out of the magnificent office. Even so, there
was a slight hesitancy in his steps, as if he wanted to be sure
he didn't stagger.

Samuel Kieller walked to the great windows and watched the old pilot climb into the single-seater moon-diver. At the last minute, one of the ground crew had to help him in. The door adjoining Kieller's office burst open and a heavy, baldish man waddled in hurriedly. "Kieller," he said, "I've been watching old Hanley walk to his ship. He's drunk. Do you think it's safe?"

"Safe?" A crafty gleam lit up Kieller's eyes. "Hanley's diving in the *North Star,* isn't he? And she's heavily insured, isn't she? What if she isn't on our schedule? What if she happens to crash because old Rugger had a shot of *behla* too much?"

"But they can get you for letting him go up in that condition!" the fat man barked. "They're liable to see right through the whole—"

"They won't," said Kieller calmly. "Because Hanley won't crash. Not *today.* Drunk or sober he's the best moon-diver on Corella, and he'll bring the *North Star* in safely. But tomorrow the *Silverbeam* comes in."

"The *Silverbeam?* Isn't Hanley's son aboard that ship?"

"You have an excellent memory, Frazer. Yes, young Ronald Hanley is our new Navigation Officer on the *Silverbeam.* Rugger will want to bring that ship in." Kieller paused, lighting a fresh cigar. "I'll have a little surprise for old Rugger tomorrow with your help," he said, showing his teeth as he smiled. The fat man sighed and smiled with him, and in silence both watched the tiny pilot craft take off.

There was a sudden roar, a flash in the rocket pit, and the ship swept into the moon-studded heavens of Corella. On the inner side of the moons, they looked like pale green and white bodies, moving harmoniously across the sky in beautiful order. But they were more than that—they were almost the sky itself because there were so many of them. The 212 moons of Corella were a curtain that separated it from the universe, a curtain with tiny holes that showed now and then. Hanley's ship had unerringly darted through one of those holes the instant it appeared.

Now he had gone up to meet the *North Star* two hundred thousand miles out, to lead it in a dive back through the moons—lead it as only a pilot craft with the Steinway Integrator could lead the way...

Forty minutes later, the eerie whine of two ships coming in together could be heard all over the spaceport of the Ceres Spaceways Company. Kieller, chewing the butt of his cigar, and Frazer, standing beside him, looked into the heavens. The great moons moved in their various orbits and speeds, some slowly, some scudding along—and suddenly there was a gap among them and two ships came diving through, easily, gracefully, swinging in in wide arcs.

When Rugger Hanley climbed out of his craft, he didn't go chat with the officers of the *North Star* the way other moon-diving pilots did. He lurched across the field, talking to no one, disappearing from sight.

"Odd fellow, that Hanley," sighed Frazer. "Sort of a hermit."

"Been that way for years," Kieller said. "Maybe he's been in the game too long. He used to be pretty lively and a good mixer until he took to drinking *behla*." He crushed the cigar butt. "Works out fine for us," he said softly. "Tomorrow, when the *Silverbeam* crashes, we'll be through for a long while. Just as well the last crash will be above suspicion."

"JUST leave the capper here with me, Nikko," said Big Mike O'Shea, the bartender. "No use trying to wake Rugger. He's full of *behla*."

The little Martian shook his head. In both hands he held tightly clasped a capsule wrapped in the yellow and blue paper that signified it came from Earth. He stood over the sleeping form of Rugger Hanley and tried to wake his master. It was long past the Corellan curfew, and the drinking house was empty. The police had cleared the place an hour before, and they let Hanley stay there only because Big Mike had said he would put up Hanley for the night.

"You hear me, Nikko?" O'Shea said as he swept the littered floor. "Leave the capper here. Rugger likes to read his son's cappers when he's sober, and it can wait until then." He approached the little Martian who refused to move. One of his large hands burrowed into the Martian's little ones and he took away the capsule from the silent Nikko. The bartender turned it around and looked at the writing on it. Suddenly his face went white. His hands relaxed and the capsule fell from his grasp.

"It can't be!" Big Mike gasped. "It can't—*Tom Worth's been dead three weeks!*"

Nikko nodded his head solemnly, and his green eyes flashed, as if he understood the shocking words. He stooped and picked up the capsule. O'Shea muttered as he shook himself. "Come on, you damned heathen Martian, we'll both of us wake up old Rugger."

A few minutes later, Rugger Hanley was sick from the stuff that Mike poured down his throat. He held his head in his hands and groaned. "I'm all right, Mike. Don't give me any more of that damned swamp syrup." He lifted his head and looked up, his eyes glazed. "Is that Nikko?" he asked. "What's little Nikko doing here?"

"Rugger," said O'Shea quickly, "you've got to listen to me. Nikko brought you a message, a capper from Earth."

Hanley nodded. "I know. Been expecting it. My son's coming in tomorrow on the *Silverbeam*. It's all over now, Mike. He's going to find out about me at last...and it's too late to help me..."

"Rugger! It isn't from your son—it's from Tom Worth!"

If old Rugger Hanley heard, he gave no indication of it. "It's over now, Mike," he went on quietly, immersed in his own thoughts. "I've won. Tomorrow my son comes in as a Navigation Officer on a great liner...but he'll find out about me... It's his first flight, and I'm washed up...too late to help me." His voice trailed off, then he went on, as if he had just heard O'Shea. "Tom Worth, did you say? He wanted to see Ronald. He loved the kid."

The bartender grabbed the jug of *neemsplant* extract that Hanley had called swamp syrup, and forced more of it down Hanley's mouth. Then he ran to the back of the bar and brought out the capsule-reader. He paused briefly when he took up the capsule, for he was breaking one of the strictest J.P. laws, but he broke open the seal. He took out the copper wire and inserted it into the reader, and touched the switch.

The mechanical diaphragm began its sensitive speaking. *"Hello, Rugger, I'm sending this to you in a roundabout way—"*

Rugger Hanley started violently. His eyes stared up into space. He half rose from his chair. "Lord!" he cried hoarsely. "Tom—Tom's voice!"

O'SHEA held his hands to the switch. He shivered involuntarily as he nodded assent and tried to meet Hanley's gaze. "Nikko brought it here. It's, a capper from Tom Worth. Listen!"

*"...roundabout way, but I'll explain that after I'm through with the important part of this message. Today is Thursday, the twelfth, and I'm going up in a few minutes to dive the Cythera through the moons..."* As both men listened, the voice seemed that of doom itself, for on the twelfth, three weeks before, Tom Worth's pilot craft and the *Cythera* had crashed in a dive. *"...but I've just discovered something funny going on around here.*

*"I can't tell you everything now, except a conversation I overheard today. You remember the way you commented on the luck the Ceres*

*Company had this year, having two big ships crash and collecting insurance worth ten times the ships' value, just when it looked like they were going broke? I heard Kieller talking today, and I think he arranged those crashes!"* There was a pause as the voice stopped, and the voice came more quickly, as if it were arguing. *"I know this'll sound crazy to you, Rugger, but I think the Claybourne and the Skybird were both his work. If my hunch is right, the Cythera is next and after that, the Silverbeam—"*

"No!" Rugger Hanley leaped out of his chair, shouting. "No, Tom—you're wrong! Not the—"

Big Mike held the switch until Hanley quieted down. He was still partially under the influence of the *behla*, and he was trembling. When Hanley nodded, Mike let the reader continue.

*"Half an hour ago, when Kieller gave me my Haydite lenses, I thought there was something wrong with them. I sent those over to you today, on the twelfth, because I'm not going to use them. I wrote you to give them to your boy Ronald as a present from me, but that was a blind, in case Kieller had the package opened. Then I asked him for my auxiliary pair of lenses, and I'll use those today.*

*"In case I don't come back, for one reason or another, have those glasses examined. I'm sure there's something wrong with them. I'm sending this capsule in a peculiar way, first to Earth, and then I'll have it trans-shipped back here to you, because Kieller asked a lot of questions when I wanted my other lenses, and he may try to trace my mail and stop it.*

*"I'll feel awful funny if I'm with you the day you get this capsule and nothing's happened. I'm laughing already. So long, Rugger."*

THE voice stopped, but the copper wire kept spinning until the rest of it had played out. In complete silence, the two men and the Martian sat there. The sweat was pouring down old Rugger's face.

"No," said Hanley, "it can't be. I've slaved too long and I've worked too hard." The quietness of his voice frightened Big Mike. " They can't do this to me," Rugger went on talking. "You know, Mike, now that my son's coming, he'll know the truth about me, and he'll be angry. He'll say I threw myself away, because I think it's too late for me now…"

But suddenly Rugger Hanley sat up straight in his chair, and his lips pressed into a tight line. "Mike!" he said, loudly. "Mike—do you realize what they've done? Do you know what those butchers have done for their money?"

O'Shea shook his head. He couldn't speak.

And now, the momentary hysteria had passed from Hanley. "My boy's on that *Silverbeam,*" he said, speaking slowly, "and he's got Tom Worth's lenses with him."

"What?"

"Yes. I didn't wait for him to come. I sent them to him that same day. I wanted him to be wearing them when he came here on his first flight."

"But they may be your only evidence against Kieller, and if—"

"Yes, Mike," Rugger Hanley nodded grimly. "If the *Silverbeam* crashes tomorrow, I'll lose the chance to avenge Tom Worth, and I'll lose my son…and my reason for living the way I've been living these three years."

"What are you going to do?" O'Shea breathed. "Weren't you planning on diving the *Silverbeam* in yourself?"

"It isn't a question of diving it in," Hanley clipped. "The ships that crashed were up against something. Maybe the lenses maybe something else. The *Silverbeam* has to be stopped from coming in tomorrow, before anything happens to her!"

"But how?"

"I'll work that out as I go. Nikko, you come with me. Mike, keep that capper here for me."

Before O'Shea could stop him, Hanley had walked, half stumbling, through the door, leaning on Nikko.

THERE were always lights at the spaceport. Day and night, no matter whether ships were expected in, the green-golden beacons lit up the great fields, the rocket pits like wounds in the smooth land. In the Communications Building, the operators were sitting, talking to the ships that were out somewhere in the void. Here the freighters, small and lonely, the gay liners, the military ships, let their voices be heard as they passed by, exchanging news, gossip, banter. The void knew no day or night...

A small terra-car drew up noiselessly beside the huge Communications Building, and a spare, unstopped figure came out. "Nikko," said the man, "wait here for me." Then Rugger Hanley went into the building. He entered an elevator and went up to the topmost story. When he came out, he was in the midst of the Section-At-Hand division, where contact was kept with the ships bound for Corella from all over the universe.

"Hi, Rugger," a short man called out to him. "What're you doing up this time of night? We haven't seen you around here in a long while."

Hanley forced a blank smile. "Hello, Charley. I'm being kept pretty busy these days." He paused. "Listen, Charley, will you do me a favor?"

Charley grinned. "Run out of *behla?* Here's a couple of bucks—"

Rugger gestured impatiently. "Thanks," he said. "It isn't that. Listen, my boy's coming in tomorrow on the *Silverbeam*. Do you think you could manage to let me get a message to him?"

"Hell, Rugger," said Charley, "I don't have to tell you that the *Silverbeam's* in the At-Hand section, and with the interplanetary clock at 22:04, most of the crew's asleep there."

"I know. Only this is something special. Could you manage to fake a navigation call, so they'll call him to the audivisor and I'll hear his voice?"

"You sure are nuts about that kid," Charley muttered. "Listen, Rugger, you know you're asking me to break all the rules? What the hell kind of a message am I going to fake? What's the hurry anyway? He'll be in within twelve hours. Can't you wait?"

"Tell him to watch out for asteroid fragments—anything, I don't give a damn. After that, there's a message I've got to give him. It may be important."

"Asteroid fragments, hmm!" Charley snorted. "If the chief ever heard me give out… Okay, I'll do it, but I must be nuts. Only remember you can't say anything personal. He'll recognize your voice, but you'll have to give him the message in third person."

"Thanks, Charley," Hanley said quietly. He could hardly conceal the fever that burned in him. The strain to keep his voice and manner casual was almost more than he could endure. He took Charley's arm and followed him into one of the cubicles whose walls consisted of great concave charts of the void around Corella. Here and there tiny pinpoints of colored lights marked the locations of ships as the lights moved imperceptibly along the charts.

"See that white one?" asked Charley, pointing. "That's it."

"Sure looks pretty."

"Look out, Rugger!" Charley grabbed Hanley by one arm. "Hell, you almost fell right on top of the speaker!" Charley frowned as he looked at Hanley. "I can smell that *behla* over here," he said, shaking his head. "Now take it easy while I get her."

CHARLEY'S hands raced over the glistening black instrument board, touching levers and pressing buttons. A red bulb glowed brightly and Charley took the speaker. "Corella Ceres Company calling *Silverbeam,*" he said once. Then he repeated it.

*"Silverbeam* in Corella Section-At-Hand," came the answer.

"Navigation warning. Is the Navigation Officer there?"

"That you, Charley?"

"Right. Hello, Fred."

"Listen, Charley, you know the whole damn crew's asleep. What the hell are you doing interrupting my reading?"

"You read too much anyway. Fred, can you get me the Navigation Officer?"

"You serious about that?"

"You're damned well told I am. You know the by-laws by now, son. Navigation warnings in person to the Officer."

"Nuts," said the voice. Then it added, *"Silverbeam* in Corella Section-At-Hand requests your line to keep open. The Navigation Officer is being called." A tiny, stifled voice added, "Nuts."

"Okay, Rugger," Charley whispered. "You take it from here." As he stood up to let Hanley take his chair, Charley said, "What's the matter, Rugger? What're you shaking like that for? Anything wrong?"

Hanley shook his head. "I'm fine," he whispered. "Just fine."

"Navigation Officer Hanley aboard the *Silverbeam* reporting," the audiphone said suddenly.

"Navigation warning," Rugger Hanley said evenly. "Unconfirmed reports of asteroid fragments. Suggest double watch all the way." He couldn't keep his hands still.

"Hey, is that—" the voice started, then stopped. "Thank you very much for the timely warning. Is that all?"

"Personal message to Navigation Officer Hanley," said Rugger. He felt Charley's hand on his arm and he shook it off. "He is requested by Rugger Hanley not to wear Haydite lenses sent him recently and to use the standard equipment of the ship. Have you got that?"

Rugger Hanley could hear Charley's sigh of relief as he gave the message impersonally. He looked up at Charley and whispered, "Get me a drink of water, Charley. I feel faint. Don't worry—I'll sign off."

The short man hesitated, then hurried through the door.

"Ronald!" Rugger Hanley said sharply. "Listen to me! You've got to get the *Silverbeam* to turn back! Don't let it land on Corella! I can't explain. Do you hear me? They're trying to sabotage the—"

"*Rugger—get away from that speaker!*" Charley had come running back into the room and he dived at Hanley. Hanley stood up and swung his free left hand, catching the short man on the chest. As Charley fell, he raised an arm and swung it across the black board. The red bulb went out suddenly. One word had come through the audiphone: "*What?*"

Charley stood up dazed. "You're crazy!" he barked. "Rugger, you've gone out of your head! Do you realize what you've done may cost me my job?" He brushed a hand across his chest.

"It may cost me more than that!" said Hanley savagely. "Charley, I can't reason with you now. I've got to get the *Silverbeam* to change her course. It's a matter of life and death for hundreds of people."

"Get out!" Charley cried. "Get out of here, you drunken fool! I'll have the police here in five seconds." His face was a mask of rage and bewilderment, and he raised a hand over the alarm signal. "Get out of here while I try to undo the damage you've done."

Slowly, Rugger Hanley backed out of the cubicle and made his way down the corridor. When he came out of the building, he entered the terra-car. "Take me to 400 Metro Boulevard," he told the driver. There was no longer unsteadiness in his voice.

"YOU did *what*, Hanley?"

"I tried to warn them over the audiophone," said Hanley. "Not more than an hour ago."

Commissioner Paige of the Interplanetary Police scowled. He was in his pajamas and he was shivering with cold as he sat with Hanley in the foyer of his home. Outside the first grey signs of the Corellan dawn were appearing. "There'll be trouble about this, Hanley," the Commissioner said, sighing. "Of course, I'll wait until I've heard of it in my official capacity. And I'll take into account the fact that you're still upset over the death of your closest friend..." he grunted, "even if you did hardly ever see him since you took to drinking."

"You mean you don't believe me?"

"Frankly, no, Hanley." Paige took on a kindlier attitude. "Be reasonable, man. How can I have the course of a liner changed on the—uh—unverifiable scraps you've given me? Where is the capsule? Your friend O'Shea seems to have left his bar and you don't know where he lives. The mysterious Haydite lenses are aboard the *Silverbeam*. All right. Let's wait a few hours. The ship will come in, and then we'll have a look at them. Maybe there has been foul play. The Department hasn't overlooked that."

"But the ship won't come in! Tom Worth was right!"

"There isn't any sense in your exciting yourself this way, Hanley. You can see I can't do anything." Commissioner Paige drew his robe on. "Isn't it faintly possible, Hanley," he said, half humorously, "that all this is just a bad *behla* dream?"

Rugger Hanley rose and clenched his fists. "I don't drink *behla,*" he said slowly. "I haven't had a pint of the stuff in the last three years you spoke of. I had some earlier tonight, when I realized that tomorrow my son would be here. It broke me up. But I don't drink."

"Ah," said Commission Paige, rising with Hanley. "So you don't drink *behla,* is it? Perhaps you can explain your constant—"

"I can't. Not unless I'm willing to give up my last chance to save that ship. And that's one thing I won't give up." He bade the Commissioner goodnight and went back to the terra-car.

After that, Rugger Hanley lay in bed awake all through the night, unable to sleep. And all the while he was thinking, planning, working the thing out in his mind. There were only a few chances for Kieller to take to gain his ends. Hanley had to know them all in advance. There must have been something he'd overlooked.

For the rest of that night, Nikko, the little Martian, sat by his bed, dozing off and awaking just in time to light Hanley's next cigarette. It was very quiet where they lived, far from Metro, far from the spaceport and the men with whom Hanley had spent so many years of his life...

THE *Silverbeam* was due in at 32:30, interplanetary time, and an hour after noon Corellan time, but Rugger Hanley got to the spaceport an hour ahead of time. Word of the past night's events had gotten around, and as he made his way slowly to the pilot craft hangars, he could feel the way people were looking at him. He felt very tired and he knew his face showed it. He had to be very careful now that everyone was watching him. There was no sign of his drinking now, and he hoped that most people would assume he was tired...because if they caught the answer...

The mechanics, with whom Hanley had seldom exchanged a word in years, clustered around him. One of them had a message. "Mr. Kieller said to be sure to see him before you go up for the *Silverbeam.*"

Rugger nodded. He had planned to see Kieller himself. In Rugger Hanley's plans, Kieller was destined to play a leading role within the hour. But he was a bit startled to hear that he had been posted to take in the *Silverbeam.* Of course, Kieller had known that Hanley would want to bring that ship in; Kieller had conferred a great favor on Hanley by signing young Ronald on one of the Ceres Company ships. But that meant that they weren't going to discipline Rugger for last night's events. Or did it mean that at all?

He had the mechanics go over the tiny pilot craft thoroughly. He was careful not to ask them more than the usual questions, not until they were all finished. Then he said, "Please check and see whether the sparkers are all set," then, hesitating, and as if he had thought it over, he added, "On second thought, get me a whole new line of sparkers."

Of course there was hesitancy; he'd expected it. One of the mechanics said, "But the ship doesn't need them, sir."

"She lost speed too fast yesterday," said Hanley. "I think—"

"But, sir," the mechanic interrupted, "you didn't use this ship yesterday at all."

"Didn't I?" Hanley said, cursing his blunder. "That's all right," he caught himself, "get a new set anyway. I'm not taking any chances today. If I could use a brand new ship, I would."

"Yes sir," said the mechanic. "It's a big day for you, isn't it?" He was a friendly youngster, that mechanic.

"Mind your business!" Rugger snapped. He was immediately sorry. He had been wondering which of these young mechanics was the one who would soon be sneaking away to report to Kieller, to tell him of the careful checkup he'd ordered, the new sparkers. One of them, certainly, and then Kieller would know. Hanley had to stop him.

WHEN the new line of sparkers had been installed, Rugger Hanley said, "Lock up the ship, please, and give me the key." The mechanic hesitated at the strange order, but he took one look at Hanley's set jaw and complied. As he gave Hanley the key, Rugger whispered, "Sorry I barked at you, son. I'm just upset."

As he made his way to the administration Building, just as he left, Hanley heard one of the mechanics say in a low tone, "The old boy's gone completely nuts. Morale shattered. Worth's crash must have…"

He wanted to walk away faster, but he kept his pace slow, his head down. There were more people at the Administration Building, standing in little knots. The news had spread fast. Hanley wondered whether it wasn't a good thing. Maybe all the publicity would stop Kieller because it would be too co-incidental.

No, it wouldn't do that at all. If anything happened now, they would be sure that Hanley had been crazy, and his unbalance had resulted in a tragedy. It was the best thing he could have done for Kieller. They could only say that Kieller might have exercised better judgment.

"Hello, Hanley. Aren't you going to talk to me?"

Rugger started. "Sorry," he mumbled. "I must have overlooked you. I'm all wrapped up in thought, Commissioner Paige."

"Come here a moment, Hanley," said the Commissioner, taking Hanley by the arm. "That's just what I want to talk to you about." He went inside the cool corridor with Hanley and stopped where they were alone. "I've been upset by the things you told me last night, Hanley. Frankly, I'm worried whether it's exactly wise for you to go up in your mental state." The Commissioner hesitated. "I've been wondering whether Kieller isn't showing more sentimentality than sound judgment in allowing you to go up today."

"Please," said Hanley, his voice barely a whisper, "stay out of this. I'm all right. I've been flying these ships for fifteen years. You know I wouldn't go up if I thought there was any reason for me not to."

"If anything happens—"

"Nothing's going to happen," said Hanley flatly. "Nothing!"

Paige smiled. "All right, Hanley," he said. "That's all I wanted to hear. If you aren't afraid... I trust your judgment implicitly. I was only worried you might show up, ah—"

"I know," said Hanley. "Drunk. I've never gone up drunk in my life." He turned away, walking down the hall. He didn't like the way Commissioner Paige had been looking at him; he couldn't take the chance.

Now that he was about to open the door to Kieller's office, the first doubt seized him. What time was it? There couldn't be much time left, and he had to act quickly and smoothly. He entered the reception loom. "Mr. Kieller's waiting," said the secretary. "There isn't much time."

Rugger Hanley walked through the door the secretary opened. Kieller stood up from his desk. "Ah, Hanley," he said, cordially, "I've been waiting to—"

HANLEY closed the door with his back and stood against it. As Kieller spoke, he withdrew his hands from his pilot's jacket. In his right hand there was a short, blue barreled electric gun. "Don't say another word, Kieller," Hanley said softy, advancing. "I haven't much time. Open the wall safe."

Kieller's eyes held fear. "Hanley, have you gone out of your—"

"Open the safe."

It was the very quietness with which Hanley said it that got Kieller. He couldn't take his eyes off the gun. They had outlawed those guns ten years before. The old rocketeers had carried them. They could make a hole through steel, quietly, in a second. Kieller opened the safe.

"Give me Tom Worth's Haydite lenses," said Hanley evenly.

"I don't know what you're talking about," said Kieller.

"I'll give you five seconds—"

The inter-office phone buzzed and a girl's voice called, "The *Silverbeam* is about to start her dive. Mr. Hanley must hurry."

"You haven't any time, Hanley," said Kieller. Hanley took a step forward. Suddenly, Kieller's voice changed, and a new light shone in his eyes. "All right, Hanley," he said. "You've got me—but you can't do a thing until you come down again. You've no time. Here." He handed over two pairs of lenses from the safe.

"So that's it," said Hanley. "That's how you got Tom. You switched both pairs on him."

"Yes," Kieller smiled wryly. "He suspected the first pair, but not the second. You know, the light from those moons is simply terrible."

Rugger Hanley went pale. The nails of his left hand tore his palm. "Who else did you use this on?" he said.

"No one," Kieller replied calmly. "I don't use the same idea more than twice, and in this case I used it once."

"What about the *Claybourne* and the *Skybird?*"

"Ah, yes. I had another little device there. I—"

"Mr. Hanley," the phone called, "the *Silverbeam* is starting her dive now. Your ship's ready. You're late."

"Hurry," said Kieller, smiling, "or the *Silverbeam* may join—"

Hanley feverishly pointed to a piece of paper. If only he'd watched the time. Someone was knocking on the door. "Coming," called Hanley. "Write that down, damn you," said Hanley to Kieller. "Write fast. Put down what you said about Tom Worth." He waited, glanced at the paper. "Now write this," he said. "'I also brought about the crash of the *Claybourne* and the *Skybird* by substituting worn lines of sparkers in their engines, causing the rockets to lose speed and slow the dives—'"

Kieller hesitated, then smiled as he continued writing. "Very bright of you, Hanley," he observed. "It's a pleasure to lose to a man like you. You've got me dead to rights."

"...and cause the pilot craft—" Hanley was dictating.

"Mr. Hanley! Mr. Hanley! The *Silverbeam* is diving! She's calling for the pilot craft!" They were kicking at the door now, hammering and calling outside.

"That's enough!" said Hanley. He grabbed the paper and ran to the door, and as he opened it, he heard Kieller call after him, "Remember a confession's worthless without evidence—"

HANLEY rushed through the office, bumping into people, ran into the corridor, putting the gun away as he ran, trying to avoid the throngs that were everywhere and not succeeding. Several porters saw him coming and formed a flying wedge for him, and he ran behind them to the ship. It was in the pit, tilted, ready for blasting. He fumbled for the key, gave it to a mechanic, then jumped inside. The door slammed behind him as he settled into his cramped quarters. He was still holding Tom Worth's lenses and the crumpled sheet of paper that Kieller had written.

He kicked over the bars under his feet, started the engine, let his hands touch the controls... The sudden shock, the lift and tear of the rockets, the noise of the blasting. Ten seconds later, Hanley slowed his speed and peered through the glassite ports. He had been so late in starting that he'd missed all the usual roles in the curtain of moons. The Steinway Integrator, taking up most of the forward control board, was flashing brightly, its calculators marking the tiny figures and letters as they changed from instant to instant.

The *Silverbeam* was probably halfway through her dive by now. He could imagine the panic that must have been inside the hearts of the men on her bridge as she dived, unable to stop, without the sight of pilot ship to take her in. The Integrator was ticking away, flashing, and the noise of the rockets were thunder in Hanley's ears. The fatigue of the sleepless night came up suddenly to threaten his skill, and Kieller's last words rang in his ears.

"Evidence." He had it. He had it with him. Some of it Mike O'Shea had, and the rest, the counterfeit lenses, Ronald Hanley had. He could get them together, but only if he lived, and only if he brought the *Silverbeam* in safely.

When he roared though the curtain, the twin suns of Corella were close together, and the moons were at their brightest. In his hurry, Hanley had forgotten to take his own lenses! But he had Tom Worth's. The lenses were made for individuals, according to their sight, but it didn't matter much to Hanley now.

He let out the rockets to their maximum speed and sat relaxed, trying to get the feel of the ship. She was going well; the sparkers had done it. How right he had been about the sparkers! Not that it had been so difficult to figure out. There weren't many places in a ship that could be quickly and effectively sabotaged that wouldn't immediately be apparent in a check-up. But one had to suspect before one could exercise caution. And Hanley had more than suspected—he had known!

Where was the *Silverbeam?* It was time he had gotten her call. And there it came. "Hello. Hanley? Thank God you're up. We're halfway down. Can you see us?"

"No. Correct direction. Those suns are too close."

"Tack three points and a half port at present speed and hold it until we hail you."

RUGGER HANLEY set the controls and took a deep breath. He didn't usually have to fish for ships; he was up there in plenty of time, waiting for them, with time to spare...

"Hello, Hanley." It was Kieller's voice, coming through the audiphone, quietly. "We're on my private line now, Hanley, and I thought I'd like to have a last chat with you. Now don't tune me out—this is important. You know that was a clever thing you did at the port today, having those sparkers changed. The only thing is, I hadn't had them touched at all. You see? I don't use the same idea more than twice."

There was a dangerous deliberateness in Kieller's voice that made Rugger Hanley's scalp tingle. "I didn't count on the sparkers at all," he was saying. "Instead—"

"Hello, Hanley!" the contact phone bawled, drowning out Kieller's voice. "Can you see us now?"

Hanley pressed his face close to the glassite. "Yes," he said, as he threw open the switch to answer. "Changing direction and getting ready to dive before you."

He touched the controls slightly and the contact phone shouted, "Hanley veer off!" He saw the dark shape flash by him suddenly and he kicked the bars until the sky was empty again.

"Did you hear that, Hanley?" came the taunting voice of Kieller over the audiphone.

"Hanley—what the hell is the matter with you? Who's in that ship with you? Stop that talking there and pay attention! You almost rammed us!"

"Can you hear that other voice?" Hanley called. A sudden flash of hope had gone through him.

"Only a mumble. What's going on? Stop it!"

"Kieller's talking to me from the port," Hanley said. "You know I can't stop that. He's throwing me off, upsetting me. Get him to stop."

There was no way to stop an audiphone voice from a spaceport. It hadn't been provided for, according to the J.P. laws, to make certain that a pilot always listened to the port instructions.

"Do you understand, Hanley?" said Kieller's voice, speaking very softly. Rugger Hanley gritted his teeth and turned the ship over in its dive, adjusting his glasses. The *Silverbeam* was a black spot against the light, and as he dove at it, the spot grew larger. Hanley's mind was in chaos. He could hardly think straight. What was Kieller saying? What had he said, in that quiet, contented voice, while the contact phone had shouted instructions from the *Silverbeam?*

"So you see, Hanley, your caution with the sparkers didn't help you," Kieller's voice returned. "What can you do without an Integrator?"

"All right, Hanley, you're well in front now," called the *Silverbeam*. "We're following, matching speed. Well done. Hold on."

There were no more than five minutes left now.

"Look at your Integrator," Kieller said, softly, his voice just at Hanley's ears. "It looks all right, doesn't it? It was all right when you went up, wasn't it? Well, it isn't anymore. I saved my special idea just for you, Hanley. *I arranged with the kind aid of Mr. Frazer, to have your Integrator unbalanced."*

SUDDENLY it hit Rugger Hanley. He had heard the words before, but he hadn't really understood them, hadn't listened, hadn't... So that was what Kieller had saved for the last! Not the lenses, not the sparkers—the Integrator—the one thing Rugger Hanley had never thought of, because he never had figured on Frazer being part of the conspiracy.

"Hanley, what are you laughing at?" the *Silverbeam* called.

Rugger threw out the contact sending phone, so his voice could no longer be heard. He was laughing almost hysterically now, and the tears were rolling down his cheeks. He was crying like a child, and then the noise stopped, and only the tears and the shaking of his shoulders showed that he hadn't stopped. He was diving now full into the moons and the *Silverbeam* was right behind him.

The moons were like great, hot balls of gold. Their light came up through his lenses and filled his brain. Rugger Hanley was quiet at last, his body motionless, his hands poised, leaping to the board and touching it, and the tiny craft danced with him. Faster, faster, the rockets blasting away, the moons rushing up, the light unbearable. A touch and the ship swerved, then swerved back again.

"All right, Hanley! Hold!" the *Silverbeam* called.

Then Corella was under him, and the moons above. The great planet was lovely to see. Rugger Hanley sat calmly now, guiding the ship in, spotting the spaceport and its huge markings. He was at home up here. He wondered whether he would hear Kieller's voice again, but be audiophone was quiet.

"Beautifully done, pilot Hanley!" the *Silverbeam* called.

IT wasn't an unusual landing, because no one knew what had happened.

The pilot craft landed smoothly, and the *Silverbeam* lay down in her cradle, giving a mild thrill to the children whose parents had taken them to the spaceport that day.

Not till Hanley stepped out of the ship did he realize that there was something unusual after all. There was a lot of noise coming from the Administration Building, and he thought there were people running out to him. Then, at his elbow, Commissioner Paige said, "He killed himself, just as the *Silverbeam* came into sight." The Commissioner paused, then said, "We had hooked up a phone on Kieller's, and we heard every word he said to you up there. The others gave you up for lost."

"But not you, sir?"

"No," said Paige, "not I. Because I knew the answer. It came to me after you blasted off, I prayed I was right. Hold tight now, here they come."

The spaceport police was fighting with the mob that surrounded the pilot craft, but they let one through, Ronald Hanley. "Dad!" he said, quietly, taking his father's hand. "I just heard."

Commissioner Paige bent over and whispered, "Take off your lenses, Hanley. You're still wearing them."

Rugger smiled and took off the lenses. The three men began walking through the space the police cleared, in the midst of the cheering, clamoring mob. The Commissioner and Hanley's son walked on either side of Rugger...

WHEN the Doctor was through, he turned to the assemblage in the large room and said, "I think it can be done. It's a badly neglected case, but it's not too late."

A great sigh went through the room. Rugger Hanley smiled and lit a cigarette. "Now that that's over, where was I?" he asked.

"You were explaining the *behla*," someone said.

"I know that voice," said Hanley. "That's Charley." He gripped the extended hand. "Well," he continued, "I had to have something to cover up the way I was stumbling everywhere. You see, when I lost my lenses on that trip through the moons three years ago, I didn't realize how it would develop. Then, when I found out I was getting blind by degrees, I knew it could be cured, but it would mean that I'd stop working. And if I stopped working, Ronald would have stopped going to school. So I kept right on."

"But how could you?"

"I didn't know if I could," Hanley replied. "I'd been diving through the moons for twelve years by then. I used to think that I knew those moons backwards. I knew everything about them, when they parted and made gaps, where it was, their orbits, speed, their pock-marks—every damned thing.

"The only really dangerous trip I made was the first time I went up. I went up alone that time. No ship was expected in. I said I was going up for a joy-ride, but I didn't know, exactly." He took a drag on his cigarette. "It turned out I was right. I couldn't read the little figures on the Integrator anymore, but I didn't need them. Those moons were my friends. As my eyes got worse, I couldn't read anything much, and I used to glance at things and pretend I was reading.

"I'd bump into people all the time. I'd fall over stones. But the one thing I couldn't miss were those moons. I couldn't see much, but I couldn't miss those moons. Even with my glasses on, they used to burn holes right through me when I came at them. And I knew them by then. So I kept on working. I knew I wasn't really taking chances, yet, and I was waiting for Ronald to finish.

"Then, yesterday, I was afraid I'd gone too long, and I'd be blind, and knowing the kind of kid Ronald was, I felt he'd never forgive me. I still didn't want him to find out, but I didn't know how to stop it. I thought maybe I'd go on buying *behla* everywhere, so people would always think I was drunk when I came stumbling along."

"You gave it away last night," said Commissioner Paige. "I couldn't believe you at first, but today, when I knew you hadn't had a drop in hours, and I saw you running into people on your way to the ship, I remembered how you hadn't seen me when you first came here. I had the answer then, but it was too late to stop you."

"And a good thing too," said Ronald Hanley.

"Mr. Hanley," said the Captain of the *Silverbeam*, "would you mind telling me what you were laughing about while we were diving? I still can't understand it."

A chuckle escaped Rugger Hanley. "You see, Captain," he said, "I realized then that Kieller had done the one thing that was calculated to be the end of any pilot—if he could get away with it, and he did, but here I was, the one man to whom the Integrator was useless, and Kieller had banked on that. He could have done anyone of a dozen other things. Oh, I thought about them all while he was talking to me up there.

"He could have hurt the rockets, the chambers, the contact phone, the control board. It wouldn't have been as simple as the device of the sparkers or the lenses, but since he was taking pains enough to throw the Integrator off—a really hard job—"

"And," interrupted Paige, "accomplished with the loving co-operation of Mr. Frazer, the only man here who could get to those things."

"Yes," Hanley agreed, soberly. "I hadn't figured on Frazer, or I'd have realized what I was up against, and how wide their field was. But when Kieller showed me how they'd wasted their opportunity, throwing off the Integrator, the irony of it almost killed me."

"Ah, yes," said the Captain of the *Silverbeam*, dryly, "it almost killed us all."

There was a noise in the back of the room. Voices were being raised. Then Hanley heard Big Mike O'Shea yelling, "But I tell you it ain't *behla*. It's Irish whiskey, good clean Irish whiskey, straight from me old mother in Ireland, and Nikko and me are going to drink with Rugger Hanley if we have to kill everyone in this room."

No one in the room was killed, after all, and they were still singing an hour later...

## THE END

# The Radio

## By PETER ARTHUR

*If O. Henry had written science fiction, chances are he would have written this story, with its "O. Henry twist" ending.*

I'VE thought it over, and decided to tell you the truth. Certainly I refused to give the police a statement. What could I tell them—the truth, too? They'd think I was crazy. And what would be the point in a false explanation? It was a case of the truth or nothing, so I kept still.

But you—you're my lawyer, and a man of education. Imagination, too, I hope, or this will be a complete waste of time. It's not the verdict, you understand; that doesn't worry me. A drowning man doesn't fuss over the fact that salt water stings his eyes. I've lost too much to care about prison.

All right; I know you're a busy man; I'll get to the point.

I was listening to the World Series. She—my wife—was in town, shopping. You remember the Series. It was three and three. Seemed important then. Now—but skip it.

It was the third inning of that seventh game. The Dodgers had one man on second, two out; and the count on Snider was three balls. Neither team had scored yet. A good game. And then the damn TV conked out. The screen just went black. The only thing I know how to fix is the fuse, and that wasn't the trouble. I tinkered a little; opened the back; tightened the tubes—nothing. I was plenty teed off. The set was almost new; had cost a bundle; and it had to pick a time like this to quit. Funny how serious little things can seem until you know better. A person doesn't know what real trouble is yet he carries on as if the world was ending. So I couldn't watch the game—was that so dammed important?

Anyway, there I was, stuck without a set. On a Sunday, so no repair shops open even if there'd been time. And you know my place, well out of town, on the El Toro Road. Twenty miles from nowhere. No neighbors I could watch with. I wanted to boot that lousy TV.

Then I remembered there was still such a thing as radio. Funny thing, though, I didn't know for sure if we even had one in the house. We hadn't listened for years. Still, it was a chance, so I searched the place. I found a portable in the spare bedroom, but it was kaput, like the TV. Probably hadn't been used for ages.

I was about to give up, when I suddenly remembered my Dad's old set—up in the attic. Nobody'd given it a thought since he died in 1935. There was just a chance it might still work; they built 'em to last in those days.

I hurried up to the attic, and sure enough, there it was, dusty and rickety—an old Atwater-Kent, remember them?

Well, I lugged it down. It had one wobbly leg, weighed a ton, and looked a hundred years old; but when I plugged the thing in, it actually worked. It had a weak, far-away sound when you tuned in, but perfectly clear. After thirty years, it played.

But when I got the old set tuned in on the game, I was mighty puzzled. It hadn't taken more than twenty minutes to find the radio, yet instead of being in, at most the fourth inning, they were in the last of the fifth.

It didn't seem reasonable, not in a World Series, where everybody takes his time, and is careful as hell. I wanted to know what I'd missed anyhow, and as usual in that case, the announcer talked about everything else, including the heights and weights of the players' grandmothers. So I phoned Jerry Martin. It didn't take him long to straighten me out. Said I was nuts. Certainly it was only the last of the fourth.

It's the truth; I can't help it. That's the way it was. That old set was exactly one hour ahead of the rest of the world! Don't look at me like that. I know it sounds crazy. But I can only tell you what happened. I'll take a lie detector test any time you say.

I didn't believe it myself, at first. But it was an easy thing to verify. I just took the radio schedules from the paper, and tuned in a dozen or so programs. Each one came on about an hour ahead of the usual time.

Well, I spent the rest of that afternoon in a daze. I knew an hour before Jerry that my bet was safe—that Los Angeles had won. I had crazy, wild dreams of money to be made on races, stocks, politics—even had ideas of doing a TV broadcast involving predictions: the old Drew Pearson gimmick, but with one hundred percent accuracy.

I didn't even wonder how Dad had done it. If he hadn't died so suddenly from that heart attack, I suppose he'd have told us plenty. As it was, the set rotted in our attic for thirty years. Now I'd be damned if anybody else would ever get it from me. Maybe the scientists could improve it; get farther into the future, and all, but my exclusive would be gone. No, I was better off with my one hour for myself.

Time began to drag about four, because I was anxious for Stephanie—my wife—to get back, so I could tell her the incredible, wonderful news. We share—shared—everything.

At five she was still out, and I was listening, in a dreamy sort of way. It was one of those nauseating programs where they set up a mike and buttonhole people going by. This was in front of a drugstore in town, one of those Hollywood places where stars are supposed to pop in. They were questioning some giggly dame they'd stopped, when all of a sudden there was a flock of excitement. A car had swerved up on the sidewalk, and hit a woman.

Naturally, they couldn't or wouldn't identify the victim on the air—some FCC rule, I suppose. But they bore down on the incidentals: how the driver looked like a maniac or drug-fiend; that the woman had been knocked out of her shoes, and lay there in her stocking feet. Her purse had been tossed near the mike, and the announcer couldn't resist describing that—a green plastic bag with a chrome monogram, SDR. When he said that, I was sick. There couldn't be two such purses, and I knew immediately that the woman was Stephanie.

Sure, I know you don't get it. Sounds completely impossible; but this is exactly the way it happened, I tell you.

I sat there stunned, nearly out of my mind. I love—loved—my wife, and now she—but I didn't know, for sure, then. There still seemed to be hope—time. You see, I remembered that my radio was still an hour fast. The accident hadn't actually happened yet!

Don't you see! There was a chance—a good one. If only I could get there in time. Head Stephanie off a block down, or stop the car that was going to hit her.

When the idea struck home, I jumped up. That's when I bumped the radio. The weak leg broke, and the whole thing crashed. If the set was only still working, you'd know I wasn't lying.

But I had no time to bother about it then. I ran to my car, started up, and drove for town like mad. Usually it's a forty minute run on the freeway, but this was the rush hour. You know what it's like: bumper to bumper at twenty miles an hour. Could I ask a cop to rush me through? Tell him I was trying to prevent an accident fifteen minutes before it was supposed to happen?

So it was damn near six ten before I got near that drugstore. Even then, I wasn't too clear about what to do. I hoped to catch Stephanie some distance off, and get her out of there.

My time was about gone, and I was in bad shape emotionally; sweat in my eyes; full of the shakes. I spotted an opening in the traffic, and stepped on the gas, heading for a parking space near the store. Then everything went wrong. That fool kid ran out into the street after his damned balloon, with his mother squawking behind him like an old hen.

What could I do? It's instinctive for a driver to avoid hitting somebody. I turned aside hard, and before I could stop, was over the curb, into the crowd, with something soft under my wheels.

I climbed out, scared and dizzy, but accident or not, worried about my wife first. The pop-eyed man by the mike was holding a green purse and shouting. Then I saw—in front of my car—and her shoes—you know the rest.

## THE END

# Traveling Companion Wanted

## By RICHARD WILSON

*To share exps., relieve at wheel—must be able to drive under grt.
pressure—in return transp. doz. mi. or so under ocean bottom!*

YOU remember Regan. He's the man who fell overboard in
a spacesuit and found that there really is a passage to India. It
winds down from the Champion Deep in the Atlantic and
comes out somewhere off Bombay. It took Regan a week to
pop in one end of that underworld river and emerge at the
other. He was delirious when he bobbed to the surface and was
picked up by the Chinese motorship. Starved, of course; had to
spend a long time in the hospital after he'd been transferred to
shore.

The newspapers and radio and television made quite a thing
of it. Reporters managed to interview Regan while he was still
weak and maybe talking a little crazy. They got together
afterward and agreed among themselves on what parts to leave
out. Then Regan sold the first-person rights to a syndicate. He
insisted on writing the installments himself, but a lot was edited
out while the staff writer was redoing it.

I didn't hear Regan's unpublished story till I met him in the
bar at the Palmer House in Chicago. He'd been attending a
geophysical meeting that I'd had to cover and we'd both got
bored with it about the same time. I thought I recognized him
from his pictures and said so. Regan seemed glad to have a
non-longhair to talk to, and he talked.

You know why Regan had been wearing a spacesuit in the
first place; he'd become something of a hero on the return trip
of one of the Earth-Mars hops after a meteor struck. Regan
went out through the airlock to make repairs. It was his job as

67

chief of maintenance. Patched up the hole and went back in. Routine, he said.

But the skipper messaged a report to Earth, and when the spaceship reached the way station to take on landing fuel, the press was waiting for it. The photographers were along and they wanted Regan to re-enact the repair scene. He didn't want to, but the skipper insisted because it would be good public relations. So Regan climbed into the spacesuit again and took along his mobile repair gear and tinkered away on the hull while the photogs snapped away from a patrol boat.

That was when the repair unit went out of whack.

ITS mobility factor wasn't supposed to do anything more than move him around on the hull to wherever he had to go. He'd worked with it a hundred times in test sessions and once in reality and it'd always been a lamb. But this time it went all screwy and shoved him off the hull. In some way one of the conduits wrapped itself around his arms like an octopus, pinning them so he couldn't reach the controls. And in some other way the tiny rocket engine zipped over to full power and plunged him down toward Earth.

If it had headed him out toward space, it would have been all right. The patrol boat could have overtaken him in a few hours at most and hauled him aboard. But Regan was heading Earthward and soon he was down where the traffic's pretty congested. The patrol boat made some valiant efforts, but after a couple of near misses with transcontinental rockets, it gave up. Better to lose one person than a couple of hundred.

Radio messages were sent to low-flying craft and ships at sea. These didn't do any good, except that a trawler was able to spot the position where Regan, in his spacesuit, smacked the water and went under. The trawler didn't have a radio transmitter. It waited a while, and when nothing came up, it put about for land. A day later, the spot where Regan had gone down was alive with would-be rescue ships, submarines and diving equipment.

But Regan never came up—not in that ocean, at any rate.

I knew this story pretty well, so Regan didn't elaborate on it. He'd blacked out, anyway, soon after he hit the atmosphere and didn't come to till he was close to smacking the surface. That's when it began to get interesting.

You've seen enough undersea movies to know what the ocean is like, so we won't go into that. This is what happened when Regan got down to what should have been the bottom:

There was a big crater there, with the bottom stretching away in all directions from the cavity—but the hole itself kept going down. Funnel-shaped, Regan said. He could see it quite clearly because he was plunging into it head down. The tentacles of the conduit were still wrapped around his arms and the mobility gadget's rocket was naturally working almost as well under water as it had in space.

After a while, it got dark, with Regan still zipping along into the depths of the funnel. He'd long since passed the stage of being merely worried; now he was scared. By this time, it was entirely black, but Regan could sense that he was being carried along swiftly.

NOT because he thought it would do any good, but because he had to do something, Regan experimented with his feet. He found that after some back-stretching calisthenics he was able to bring his right boot up near his waist. Maneuvering it with total disregard for his sacroiliac, Regan managed to hook the boot under one of the coils the conduit had made around him. Gradually he was able to loosen it enough to give his left arm some play and from there it was relatively simple. He switched off the rocket engine, switched on his headlamp and looked around.

Regan said it was quite a sight, in a reverse sort of way. Nothing anywhere. With the rocket turned off, he kind of floated around aimlessly, going nowhere in particular. He should have been going up, but that didn't happen. He swirled like a lazy eddy. A school of things that were caricatures of fish—big, white, revolting things—swished over and puckered blindly into his faceplate, then went away. Otherwise there was nothing.

Regan was pretty discouraged. By this time, he'd been in a slow spin for so long that he had no idea which way was up. He had the equipment for getting up—there were about two hundred hours of fuel in the rocket engine strapped to his back—but no way seemed any better than another.

He remembered that the funnel had steadily narrowed and so he tried experimental bursts from the engine to see if he could reach one of the sides. Eventually he got to something that wasn't water. It was a sort of mud. Regan studied the markings on it for a possible clue. No go. Regan was a spaceman, not an oceanographer.

So, since it was better than doing nothing, Regan got himself into a drift parallel with the mud side and switched on his rocket.

He whizzed along at a good rate, staying close to the mud wall, but not knowing whether he was going down, up or around in circles at the same depth. After what he judged to be some hours of this, the mud began to be streaked with a gray substance and, still farther along, it appeared to become rock. Regan didn't know whether this was good or bad.

More hours went by, apparently. Regan was wearing a watch, but it was hidden under the heavy sleeve of his spacesuit. He dozed off, he said, and when he snapped back into consciousness he noticed that there was another wall, far off, opposite the one he was rocketing along.

It was gray, too, as far as he could make out in the light of his head lamp, which was weak over distances. What woke him up fully was something that went skimming past him at a much greater rate than his own. It was a cask, its wood brown as if from long submersion and its hoops rusted into redness. The cask was turning lazily end over end, but it outdistanced him and disappeared ahead as he watched. It had been traveling out in the middle of the passage.

REGAN pondered this for a while and then reasoned that there was a swift current, swifter in the middle even than his rocket propulsion at the side of the channel. He worked himself out toward the center, then switched off his rocket, experimentally. By watching the rock side of the passage, he was able to gauge that he was moving much faster.

The watching, however, had a hypnotic effect on him and Regan felt himself dozing off. He tried to fight it but reasoned finally that there wasn't much point. So he turned off his headlamp and let himself go to sleep.

He felt weird when he woke up. He was hot and sweating. He remembered instantly where he was. It was no comfort to him. He felt entirely hopeless, even more so than if he'd been marooned in space. At least there was traffic out there. Here there was just himself, with a wooden cask up ahead and nightmarish fish somewhere behind.

He also felt weak. Spacesuits come equipped with water, of course, if they're the repair variety, and Regan drank sparingly through the tube at the base of his faceplate. But his suit carried no rations, so he tried to ignore his hunger.

He drowsed again and switched off his headlamp. This became a pattern for him—a semi-conscious nightmare of smooth, eerie motion, punctuated with sips at his water supply and hopeless watching through the faceplate, blinking away the sweat. Regan talked to himself, he said, and sometimes sang, to keep himself sane in the silence and loneliness. It probably helped, although some of his talk was pretty idiotic.

It was after one of his dozes—whose duration he had no way of measuring even by his thirst and hunger, which were constant—that he awoke to something new. Automatically he switched on his headlamp, then switched it off again, realizing what the newness was.

The passage he was being washed through was no longer dark; there was a radiance in the water now.

Regan twisted himself around to see what the light came from. Up ahead, apparently. As it got stronger, his eyes began to ache. It was a gorgeous ache, Regan said, and he stared ahead almost hypnotized. He made an effort and focused on the walls of the passageway he was being thrust along. They were white with streaks of black in them—like marble, but without marble's glossy hardness. He could see all parts of the tunnel now; it was roughly circular and had narrowed to a diameter of about two hundred feet.

Regan could only suppose that he was nearing the surface—that he'd been sweeping through some U-shaped fissure—and he adjusted himself kinesthetically to the theory that he was now traveling up instead of down. This took a lot of doing and occupied his mind.

His spirits soared with his imagined ascent and he could visualize himself traveling faster and faster until, with a pop, he would be thrust into the air and fall back to float on the surface. Regan wanted most desperately to be able to look at the sky again. It would be kind to see land, too, but a ship or a plane would do temporarily.

HE was half-lost in this reverie when he had to make a second adjustment. Remember, he thought he was going up, as from the bottom of a well. Therefore he was puzzled, as the radiance increased to daylight strength, to see one wall of his tubular, water-filled prison darken to deep green while the other turned a sort of blue-white-pink.

He was moving in the same swift rush of current, his body positioned so that he was facing the green half. He twisted as if to face the opposite way in an elevator and then became giddy when the entire concept of his surroundings did a ninety-degree flop.

In that split second, Regan realized that he wasn't traveling vertically, but horizontally.

The well he had pictured himself in now took on the aspect of a river, with the bright blend of colors the sky, and the deep green the river bed. The banks of the river were above him. Regan gave himself a tiny rocket assist to rise.

He wasn't at all prepared for what he saw. Far away beyond the green plain through which the river was racing was a city.

Unmistakably it was a metropolis of Man, not towering or turreted, but massive and with a relative newness, which spoke of life. And as he had this thought, he could see other, smaller dwellings closer by, one-storied and circular, in a variety of colors.

He noted then that the level of the river was higher than that of the land—that the marble-like banks, which channeled the racing water, had become a transparent, glasslike substance, which rose and curved in a seemingly endless archway. The torrent completely filled the half-transparent tube, flowing smoothly so that he almost had the sensation of flying above the ground.

Regan maneuvered toward the top and from there he saw the road. It paralleled the river and ran in a straight line as far as he could see. While he watched, a vehicle sped along it from behind, paced beside him and then pulled ahead. The driver was only vaguely visible, but he had a reassuringly human appearance. The man in the car, which was a three-wheeled, boxlike affair of brilliant yellow, looked neither left nor right.

Regan yelled instinctively and waved. The cumbersome motion turned him over on his back. Opportunistically, he studied the sky from his new position, but could make nothing of it. There were no clouds, only the blue-white-pink brightness that seemed to extend to infinity.

SOMETHING flashed across his field of vision. Regan caught only a glimpse of it, then reasoned that it must have been a bridge, spanning the enclosed river. He twisted himself around to a prone position and tried to think constructively.

Somewhere there had to be an exit to this land. For his sake, there had to be, although of course this guaranteed nothing. But surely these people made use of this abundant supply of water. It would be fresh and good to drink after its long passage through the Earth, despite its source in the salt ocean. They would use it for irrigation, probably, and perhaps somewhere it was channeled for transportation—of a more comfortable kind than his own. And they might use it for power. Certainly its rushing strength would be tapped.

This thought scared him. He pictured a giant hydroelectric plant into which he would be swept and in the bowels of which his body would be mangled by the blades of a turbine.

He had to slow his mad passage. He maneuvered the equipment attached to his spacesuit and pointed the rocket exhaust ahead of him. He flicked on the power and felt his speed being cut. The powerful current pressed from behind him like a live thing, but the rocket thrust was strong, too. His progress slackened to the pace of a canoe.

Balancing himself behind the makeshift braking apparatus was difficult, both because the torrent threatened constantly to turn him end for end, and because his strength was only a memory of itself. But somehow Regan managed to achieve an equilibrium, which allowed him to look about and reassure himself that the city was still there. Its position had shifted on the horizon to a point slightly behind him, but there apparently was no end to the expanse of this underground world. The road was there, too, still parallel to the roofed-over river.

A surge of hope went through him as he spotted a man walking along the road.

Regan braked himself still further, until his speed matched that of the man. The man's costume was a brief one—knee-length trousers, a vest-like garment over a white skin, and sandals—so apparently—the climate was tropical.

Regan stared hard at the man, mutely begging him to turn. Both Regan's hands gripped the rocket tube; he didn't dare let go to wave. Then, as though he had been reached telepathically, the man looked in Regan's direction. Regan couldn't make out his expression, but apparently it was one of disbelief. The man stopped, took an indecisive step and then ran toward the river. He jogged alongside it and now Regan could see his face clearly.

IT was an intelligent face—round, broad-nosed, the eyes almond-shaped and the hair abundant and black. The man's body was stocky and powerful, graceful as he ran beside the tubed-in river. He waved and smiled, and Regan hoped his own answering smile was visible behind the faceplate of his spacesuit.

Regan doubted that telepathy had anything to do with making the man notice him originally; nevertheless, he thought furiously, *"How do I get out of here?"*

The response was made more to Regan's obvious predicament than because of thought transference, he was sure; at any rate, the man pointed, then raced ahead.

Regan lost sight of him for an agonizingly long minute or two then saw him again, standing and pointing up. Another bridge was spanning the river. The man gestured to it emphatically, then pointed ahead again and held up two fingers. Alternately he pointed to the bridge and gestured with his fingers. Regan decided that this meant there would be some sort of help for him at the second bridge beyond. He nodded his head vigorously.

The man seemed to see the motion. He nodded and smiled.

Regan cut the power of the rocket engine and let the current speed his journey. The man outside increased his own pace, and when another bridge swept overhead, he nodded and held up one finger. Regan trembled with relief at this confirmation of the pantomimed message. He fought back the weariness that had begun to creep over him again, and clung doggedly to the rocket whose exhaust regulated his speed to that of the running man.

Regan thought the bridge would never be reached. He felt supremely weary. He was sopping wet, his eyes kept going out of focus, his throat ached, and his head was throbbing with jagged pains. It took all his waning strength to cling to consciousness.

FINALLY the bridge was in sight; then overhead. The running man pointed up. Beyond the bridge, the glasslike covering ended.

Regan was out of the tunnel.

The river widened now and its velocity eased. But the current was still a powerful one. Regan pointed the rocket tube so that it thrust him upward. His rubber-and steel-clothed head broke the surface. He felt a surge of freedom.

In his joy, Regan lost control of the rocket-brake and was twisted crazily about. Instinctively he shut off the power; he was swept ahead. As the river whirled him forward, he saw the man on the bank point ahead to the right, wave him on and gesture that he would catch up later.

It was with relief that Regan let himself be carried forward by the strong current. He was traveling out of the mainstream now. In a few minutes, the river was so broad that he seemed to be barely moving, but this was merely an illusion of contrast.

Then Regan saw the mesh fence. It was a giant strainer across the river, apparently fashioned to prevent debris from being carried into the structure, which straddled the river beyond—without doubt the hydroelectric plant whose existence he had dreaded.

Regan was swept into the fence. It gave, cushioning the shock, and he pulled himself along it toward the bank. He reached it but lacked the strength to pull himself onto land.

Nearby, hugging the huge mesh fence, was the cask, which had passed him back in the dark of the tunnel.

Just as Regan was passing out, he saw the stocky man in the knee-length shorts come into sight, running as fast as he could make his legs pump.

WHEN Regan came to, he found himself being carried on the back of an open truck. He was lying there like a sack of cabbages, being bounced around as the truck sped over a bumpy road. His undersea friend was squatting next to him on the bed of the truck, holding onto the side to keep from being jolted off.

He smiled when he saw that Regan had regained consciousness and patted the chest of the spacesuit. He pointed in the direction the truck was going, but Regan was flat on his back and weak and couldn't turn to look. The jolting was making him sick.

The road became smoother and soon they entered the city. Regan said it was the damnedest place he ever saw. Everything looked like a beehive. He meant that literally, he said. All the buildings were circular, with doors down at the base and no windows. They were all different sizes and all colors. Some of the bigger ones towered up pretty high, but just how high was hard to say. They weren't built in stories, but in one continuous curving line from bottom to top.

The truck would pass through a square or a park now and again and the buildings in the distance looked like a mass of soap bubbles, all pastel colors under that blue-white-pink sky. The truck stopped in front of a big yellow beehive. Now that he was close and not being jolted around, Regan could see that the building was constructed of a kind of oversized bricks, about a foot square. They weren't joined with mortar, as far as he could tell. Apparently their own weight and shape held them together as they rose up and formed a dome. And the color was within the bricks, not painted on.

Two men, taller than his friend, came out of the building carrying a plank. They loaded Regan onto it and carried him stretcher-fashion into the building. The friend tagged along behind.

There was a sort of anteroom inside, with a man at a desk. The bearers stopped while the man took down a gadget that looked like a chessboard with buttons and pushed down half a dozen of them. Then he held out the board to Regan's friend, who pushed down some of the buttons in a different combination. After that the little friend went away, first patting Regan on the chest and smiling.

Regan was carried into a rotunda in the center of the building. The floor rose and took them to the top level. The bearers carried him off to the side and he saw the floor drop down again. They took him to a windowless room, which had light radiating from the walls, and dumped him off the plank-stretcher onto a high stone table. Regan climbed down. He supposed they were being as gentle as possible, considering his great weight in the spacesuit.

Regan's weight also manifested itself to him. He felt the heaviness of a person who has been buoyed up for a long time in water, but is now on land.

ALL this happened, except for the clank as he was set down, in complete silence. He was entirely isolated from outside sound, of course.

He lay there, feeling less sick but still hot and dizzy, trying to compose his stomach. After a while, he felt calm enough to drink a little water through the tube inside the faceplate.

A rotund man wearing a kind of white tunic came into his field of vision. Regan could see him only from the waist up. Like the friend he had met at the river, this man had abundant black hair. But his face was fat, with puffy cheeks and sagging jowls. He was much older. His hands were pudgy. He waggled them in what might have been a gesture of delight or greeting; it was hard to say which. His expression was one of pleasure. He stood at Regan's side and smiled at him. His hands felt over the headpiece of the spacesuit, then went thumping down the rest of it.

"I'll be out of the damn thing soon," Regan thought. But apparently it was too much for the fellow. Regan tried to gesture to the fastening at the back of his neck to show how it was done, but he was unable to raise his arms. He realized then how exhausted he was.

The rotund man in the tunic patted him on the chest—pit seemed to be a universal gesture—and went away.

Regan felt at peace in the room. He felt that now he was going to be taken care of and that everything, somehow, was going to be all right. He went to sleep.

He woke up ravenously hungry. He seemed to be alone in the room. His encased body felt as heavy as the whole world. He tried to raise up to bring his mouth to the water tube. He couldn't. He cried out in a voice that was weak even inside the confines of his suit. No one could possibly have heard and no one came. He tried to raise his arm. The muscles strained and quivered. By using all his strength, he was able to lift it a few inches above the table. Then the arm fell back on the stone with the barest tap of sound.

The jovial fat one reappeared. He was carrying a metal box with two dials on it and wires coming from it, which ended in kinds of suction cups. He stuck one of the cups to Regan's faceplate, fastened another one to his ear and twirled a dial.

"Please get me out of this suit," Regan said.

The man's face lit up with pleasure. He nodded and patted the chest of the suit. Then he spoke.

The language was a guttural, fast-paced one. Regan had never heard anything like it.

"Please," he said. "Please get me out."

The man continued to smile. He beckoned and two other men appeared. They took turns listening to Regan plead to be released. They smiled, too, though obviously none of them understood a word. Without gestures, it was impossible for Regan to convey his plight.

THEY stood around him, chattering in their outlandish tongue. Others joined them. They all had the same look about them. Friendly, smiling faces and hands that patted him on the chest. It became a confused nightmare as still others streamed in, as if he were the main attraction in a fifty-cent tour.

But apparently there was method in their milling around. They measured him from top to toe, from side to side, in circumference and in depth. They used steel tapes and calipers and jotted down their findings in little books or punched them out on button-studded chessboards. They wheeled in a huge contraption, which must have been a camera and clicked it at him from every angle. They lifted his arms and legs and chattered with excitement to see how peculiarly he bent at the joints.

It was as if Regan were a new kind of animal that had swum into their ken and which they were classifying, or which they would classify at their leisure after they had measured it in all possible ways.

They kept it up for an eternity and a half. Regan's vision got hazy, his throat burned and his stomach ached in irregular spasms.

He was barely conscious when the two bearers came back in, loaded him on the plank and took him out into the rotunda. The throng of scientists followed. The floor-wide elevator sank to the main level and they all went out into the street.

A big, rectangular, doorless, buslike vehicle was standing there. The bearers, with a great deal of effort, propped Regan up in the front seat. His head lolled back inside the suit. The shift in position blacked him out temporarily. He came out of a period of nausea to hear himself saying over and over:

"You open it at the back of the neck. I'd do it myself if I could move my arms. You open it at the back of the neck."

The bus was in motion. It rumbled through the streets among the pastel beehives. In Regan's state, they were so many bouncing balloons being pointed out by madmen in white smocks in a caricature of a vehicle under an impossible sky.

They eventually reached a kind of park or estate. Shrubs and trees were neatly set out and a big golden beehive stood at the end of a long drive. They took him inside, half fainting, sweating, gibbering to himself.

Through half a dozen anterooms they went, to what could only have been a throne room. It was sumptuously hung with tapestries. There were guards standing at post and a thick carpet led to a dais on which were two huge chairs. A tall, slender, dark-haired man sat in one of them. The other was empty.

There was a confused kind of ceremony in which everyone got down on one knee before the man on the throne, and a ridiculous struggle began, to get Regan into a semblance of the same position.

The king, or whatever he was, gestured, and Regan found himself being dragged up on the dais and sat on the other throne.

Then the nightmare took a turn for the worse. From an anteroom came a procession of women bearing gifts. They were the first women Regan had seen in this underground world, but he was less interested in them than in what they carried.

Food.

Baskets of fruit.

Platters of meat.

Cups of liquids.

The smiling creatures curtsied before the thrones and set out the feast in front of Regan. One of them, dressed in a single pale blue garment belted at the waist, laid a basket of fruit in his lap.

Regan began to quiver in a fever of frustration.

It got worse when, at a sign from the king, everyone helped himself to some of this or that, raised it to Regan in a kind of toast and began to eat.

If any of them noticed that Regan didn't join them, they were polite enough not to take offense.

THE feast over, everyone went for an after-dinner ride. The king went, too, riding in a richly draped palanquin on wheels, ahead of the squared-off bus.

This was the royal tour. Points of interest were visited. Regan's bleary eyes and uncomprehending brain half observed gardens, factories, schools, a sporting event, a parade, a farm and dozens of examples of the culture of the world of people who were kindly starving him to death.

In his semi-delirium, he once reproached himself for being such an unappreciative guest and wondered what they must think of this emissary from outside who was such a cumbersome clod. He had come to them in the strange trappings he apparently preferred, so how could he blame them for respecting his costume and leaving it to him to wear it or remove it as he chose? In his own world, he wouldn't strip a visitor or skin a stray dog.

A bump in the road and the shudder it gave the bus jolted his eyes fully open. Ahead was the hydroelectric plant spanning the river. They were going to show the king where Regan had come from.

The procession pulled over to the bank next to the mesh fence, which screened debris from the water flowing into the plant. On the bank lay his mobility unit, which apparently had been detached before they trucked him into the city originally. The king got out of his palanquin and examined it curiously. Then he got back in and they drove along the bank to the other side of the hydroelectric plant. The river continued its swift passage, apparently unslowed by the drain on it.

Regan thought the river looked tremendously inviting. In its depths, he could be free of the well-meaning crowd of sightseeing guides. The river represented peace, an end to being shown around, measured, observed, exhibited and tantalized. In it, he could die calmly, without any frustrating diplomacy.

A bridge spanned the river below the plant. By the gestures of the scientists, he gathered that they were going to cross over to see interesting things, which lay across the river. The bridge was a narrow wooden one. Parallel to it was the stone framework of an unfinished replacement. They proceeded slowly over the rickety, railless bridge.

The approach to it was banked, so that Regan was tilted in his seat, toward the outside. The bus leveled off as it reached the wooden planking and Regan tilted the other way. A loose plank under a wheel sent him swaying back again. With all his remaining strength, he leaned with the tilt. It was just enough to send him off balance.

They reached out to pull him back, but it was too late. He was out of the bus and dropping the short distance to the water.

The current was so swift that he went only a little way under, then bobbed up and was rushed along, turning over and over. As he revolved, he caught glimpses of consternation on the bridge. He saw the bus back off and race along the road on the bank, hands waving out of it. But it couldn't catch up with him. He was moving too fast.

The even motion of the river was soothing. Regan took a swallow from his tube and relaxed. There was a dull ache in his stomach, but no more stabbing spasms. Maybe he was dying. He didn't care.

REGAN knew he was in a hospital even before he opened his eyes. The ether-and-disinfectant smell told him that.

It was taking an effort to thrust his eyelids up. He moved his arms and felt them close to his body. He raised one hand to his face and rubbed his closed eyes. Of course they'd have got him out of the spacesuit.

He opened his eyes.

A brown-faced man was leaning over the bed. He was wearing a white smock and had a fountain pen in the breast pocket. Beyond the man—the doctor—there was a window. A perfectly ordinary window, through which Regan could see the sky. A blue sky with white clouds in it.

The doctor smiled at Regan and said in English: "How do you feel, son?"

Regan tried to speak but couldn't.

"This is Bombay," the doctor said. "Bombay, in India. It must be quite a surprise to you, but I'm glad to say you'll be all right."

"What?" Regan asked vaguely.

"It's strange, of course," said the doctor. "You should be on the other side of the world, by all that's natural. We communicated with the American authorities when we saw your identification. It is extremely odd. Still, here you are, and you will be well. Quite soon, too."

"But—" Regan began. Then he gave up. He said nothing more until after he'd eaten and slept and the doctor asked him if he felt strong enough now to see the reporters.

"TWO more, sir?" the bartender at the Palmer House asked. I nodded.

"Naturally they thought I was delirious," Regan said, "or had been. They had to accept the fact that I'd been through the Earth. Not through the center of it, or anywhere near it—they tell me that's practically solid nickel, or molten, or whatever. But there was no disputing that I'd gone down in the Atlantic and come up in the Indian Ocean. They'd seen me go down and they'd seen me come up and obviously I'd been somewhere in the interval. I hadn't walked, that was for sure.

"They credited my story of the underground river. The Greeks had a word for it, they tell me. The Greeks thought the Alpheus River wandered down under the Adriatic and came up in Sicily. I don't know much about their river, but mine apparently follows the Earth's curve maybe a dozen miles below the surface.

"But nobody wanted any part of my story of the city and the king and the beehive houses and the rectangular bus. Delirium, they said. Oh, they were kind about it, but they said it. So did the geophysical boys upstairs, in their eight-syllabled way."

The bartender brought fresh highballs, but Regan still held the glass the old drink had been in. He put it on its side on the bar and stared at the open end. I got the image—a tunnel filled with rushing water, a tunnel under the world.

Regan almost echoed my thoughts.

"Tunnel under the Antarctic," he said half to himself. "That's where it must have been—that city. Down there, deep under the ice. Used to be tropics, you know."

"The Antarctic?" I said.

"Before the ice came, before the Earth's axis shifted. Those people—they didn't evacuate, I guess. They went underground. Funny they should have built themselves houses the same shape as those of the Eskimos who stayed aboveground in the North—like igloos. But probably that's just coincidence. You don't find igloos in the tropics. I'd guess their beehive houses are naturally influenced by the cavern they live in—their little universe."

REGAN looked up. He grinned and set the empty glass upright on the bar. "I've had a lot of time to think about it. They're awfully nice people, all of them. I could have had a wonderful time if I'd been able to climb out of that damn spacesuit. In time, I could even have communicated with them passably well. Good-looking women, too."

He looked at me speculatively. He opened his mouth as if to speak again, then smiled and shook his head.

I said it for him: "You're going back."

"Yes," he answered. "Yes, I'm going back. I know the coordinates of the entrance to the passageway and its dimensions and the kind of equipment I'll need. Nothing elaborate. In another year or so, I'll have enough saved up, I think. Get myself a little space launch; one of the smaller ones, lifeboat size. Fit it out with food and water—and some picture books, of course, to show them what it's like where I come from. I'd take somebody along with me if I could find anyone who wanted to go—and who believed me."

"I believe you," I said. "But—"

"Sure. You'd be crazy to go. Wife and kids. I've got none of that. Mostly what I want to do, I guess, is prove those longbeards upstairs are cockeyed."

"I hope you do. Maybe you'll let me write about it when you get back."

"It'll be a good story," Regan assured me.

"I'll be waiting for it," I promised.

That was five years ago. Four years ago, Regan went, as he said he would. He went alone, in a little space launch.

I'm still waiting to write the end of the story.

## THE END

# The Case of Jonathan Lane

## By DAVID WRIGHT O'BRIEN

*It was a terrible injustice—but when Jonathan Lane found another had stolen his body, he accepted the strange trade.*

WHEN I opened my eyes to stare bewilderedly at the cracked, filthy stretch of yellowed ceiling above me, and turned my aching head to one side, surveying the dingy, squalid surroundings of the little room in which I lay, some sixth sense made me instantly aware that this was not a dream.

I threw the coarse, thin blanket that had covered me quickly to one side and sat up sickly, unbelievingly, both hands gripping the rusted sides of my decrepit iron cot.

My brow was cold with sweat, and my heart hammered swiftly in some inexplicable excitement. I felt somehow, and the word does not precisely—fit, as if I were *alien* to myself.

An elevated train clattered swiftly beneath the soot-covered single window of my room, shaking the very foundations of this ugly frame dwelling so that the cot on which I sat squeaked protestingly until it had passed.

I rose then, and moved almost dazedly to the washstand in the corner of the room. There was only one faucet, and its greenly discolored brass handle bore the faint, grease-caked legend "Cold."

It wasn't until I had turned on the faucet and splashed my burning face vigorously in the icy water that I had the courage at last to look full into the mottled square of mirror above the bowl.

I had never seen the reflection in that mirror before in my life. Never. I stared speechlessly, strickenly.

A stranger, open-mouthed and wide-eyed in horrified astonishment stared back at me from that mirror.

And now I knew—knew with nauseous certainty the hideous truth at which my sixth sense had hinted from the moment I'd opened my eyes to find myself in this utterly unfamiliar room.

I, Jonathan Lane, was not only inhabiting strange surroundings in a crawling room of some never-known tenement dwelling; *I was living in the body of a stranger!*

For an eternity I stood there weakly, clutching to the edge of the washbowl for support, while my mind teetered on the brink of unbridled insanity.

"This is a nightmare," I told myself. "A horribly realistic travesty of actual existence!"

And the choking whisper, which came to mock my ears, was the alien voice of this strange new body I now possessed.

"I am Jonathan Lane!" I cried hoarsely.

The very sound of this new voice derided my words. Even though my teetering sanity knew that just the night before I had been reading quietly in the study of my mansion estate...

IT HAD been close to midnight, and for the several preceding hours I'd been lost in a fascinating volume of philosophy.

Kermit, the butler who had served my father so faithfully through the years until his death—and who now watched over me with such constant, equally religious devotion—entered the study so quietly that I was unaware of his presence until he spoke.

"I have prepared your room, sir."

I looked up, startled. Then I smiled.

"Thank you, Kermit," I told him. "You quite disapprove of my burning the midnight oil, don't you?"

Kermit's tired old face registered mild rebuke.

"I was only thinking, sir—" he began.

"Of my own good, eh, Kermit?"

"For the last week or so, sir, you have had very little sleep," he began tactfully. "Rest is essential to anyone, sir."

I grinned. Little sleep was an understatement. Night clubs, cafes, bars and bistros, I'd made them all in an unceasing binge during the past two weeks. There'd been little time for sleep on that program. This night was the first one I'd spent at home, and its drastic contrast to the previous evenings marked a sudden dulling of my taste for the alcoholic hilarity of those rounds.

I turned another page and nodded to Kermit.

"Good enough, old fellow," I told him. "I'll be up to the restful comforts of my downy bed when I finish this chapter."

The solution, or compromise, seemed suitable to Kermit, and he nodded, turning to leave.

"I've prepared a hot tonic dose for you, sir," he said. "I shall leave it by your bed."

I thanked him, then, but it was considerably longer than just another chapter by the time I finally went up to my bedroom. I think I must have read through at least another four, and by the time I entered my room, it was somewhere around three o'clock.

For all the fatigue I should have felt from the constant round of dissipation of the past two weeks, I was still unable to get directly to sleep.

It must have been all of another hour that I lay there in the enormous teakwood four-poster, wide-eyed in the darkness, my mind refusing to heed the commands of a spent physical reservoir.

Nothing more than sheer exhaustion finally brought the dark curtain of sleep to me at last...

AND now I stood there, in this dingy room, surrounded by squalor and filth and poverty. Stood there in the body of a man I'd never seen before in my life. Stood there less than ten hours after I had retired to the luxurious comfort of my bedroom as Jonathan Lane, wealthiest young man in the Middle West.

Some unrealized courage now forced me to steady myself, to take hold before I gave way to utter hysteria.

With effort that brought forth renewed sweat to my forehead, I forced from my mind all but the immediate task in hand—an estimate of this nightmare in which I now found myself.

For several minutes I stared at the regular, clean-lined features of my new face. It was a face of a man about my own age before this transformation. It was not an unpleasing one. Keen gray intelligent eyes, a mouth both strong and capable of laughter. Blond hair. My own hair had been dark, almost ebon-black. The body was of medium size, sturdily built, not nearly as given to softness of muscle as my other body had been. There was a suppleness, a sense of dexterity in the fingers on the hands of my new body. They were strong, slim, brown hands. The hands of a skilled manual scientist rather than a mechanic.

Then, still forcing the grim implications of this incredible transformation from my mind, I set about examining the sordid little room.

There were clothes on a chair. Cheap clothes, frayed and worn to a pitiful shine. I quickly ascertained that these were the clothes that would have to adorn this new body of mine.

In one of the pockets of the miserable suit on the chair, I found a wallet. Opening it with hands that trembled, I saw that it contained three grubby-looking dollar bills, some eighteen cents in change, and several identification cards.

The first identification card was an employee's slip from a small chemical plant I'd never heard of. It was made out to the bearer, one Carl Gelsing.

The second was an identification slip from a currency exchange. It, too, was made out to a Carl Gelsing.

There was a snapshot half hidden behind the cards, and as I brought it out into the light, it proved to be a pose in which a smiling young man stood on a riverbank with his arm around a pretty young girl. The expression on her lovely face as she looked up at him was clearly indicative of worshiping devotion. On the face of the young man, however, there was something behind his smile that showed no real answering devotion. Something that showed instead a fierce, burning, restless ambition before which no girl, no matter how lovely could hope to stand.

I realized then, that the young man with his arm around the lovely girl was the one in whose very body I now stood!

I PLACED the picture gently back into the wallet, and returned the wallet to the suit coat pocket. Then I searched relentlessly through the only remaining object of furniture in the little room, a low, scarred dresser in the corner.

My search revealed nothing but a clean, frayed shirt that had been mended several times beneath the arms, a few socks, underthings, handkerchiefs. Nothing more. Except that the laundry marks on the personal possessions were all "C. G."

I went to the window, then, and stared down at the elevated tracks running along endlessly in either direction less than fifteen feet below. I was aware, of course, that this was a tenement sector, but precisely where it was I had little idea.

Then I began to dress myself in the frayed garments of the person who had once inhabited the body I now possessed. My actions were instinctively designed to keep myself more concerned with the results of this incredible enigma than with the madly impossible fact itself.

Once dressed, I hesitated, and all my will power was suddenly inadequate against the rising surge of mad panic that claimed me.

I don't know what might have followed, what I might have done, if a knock hadn't sounded on the door at that instant. A knock followed by a light, feminine voice.

"Carl! Oh, Carl!" the voice cried cheerfully.

The tide of panic inside me seemed suddenly to ebb. That voice had given me a brief but vitally necessary link with sanity, with reality.

Somehow I managed to answer. "Yes?"

I waited, heart hammering.

"It's Gloria, you idiot. Are you dressed yet?"

I took a deep breath.

"Yes," I said. "I'm dressed. Just a moment."

"Hurry. The restaurant will be too crowded to get service in another ten minutes," the feminine voice cried out once more.

I stepped over to the door and slid the bolt free. Then I opened it.

The lovely dark-haired girl of the wallet snapshot stood there smiling at me!

Foolishly, I stood there, groping for something to say, for any little action that would— Suddenly, and with no conscious realization of planning to do so, I bent and kissed the girl lightly on the mouth.

"Gloria," I heard myself saying. "Gloria!"

Her arms were suddenly tightly twined around me, and her mouth pressed hard against mine. The faint perfume of her hair was somehow dizzying, and her lips intoxicatingly sweet.

"Carl," she sobbed. "Oh, Carl. Are you all right? Are you really all right? You haven't done anything, have you? You haven't planned anything foolish, have you?"

I held her back from me then. "What do you mean?" I demanded. My voice was harsh with urgency.

THE girl seemed to falter. Her red lips parted as she groped for words.

"It's just that, that last night you acted so strangely, Carl," she said. "You acted as if, as if you'd never see me again, or, or…" She couldn't finish. Tears came to her eyes.

"I'm here," I heard myself saying. "I'm here and nothing has happened, has it?" *Oh God,* I thought, *nothing happened! That was richest irony!*

The girl reached into her purse then, with a sudden gesture that was completely unexpected. She brought forth a key on a string.

"Here, Carl," she said. "Here is your key. You told me to hold it for you until morning. You told me to give it to you then, if, if, you were all right."

My bewilderment was genuine. "My key?" I blinked.

"Your basement laboratory key," she said, frowning. "Don't you remember? Oh, I know you drank last night, Carl. But I didn't think you'd had so much you—"

I cut her off, not wishing to betray myself further.

"Of course," I said. "Now I recall. Thanks." I took the key.

She turned then, saying, "Come, we'll have to hurry."

"Hurry?" I said the word without thinking.

"Yes, if we want to catch coffee and rolls before work."

"Oh, yes," I managed. "Work. That's right."

The girl whirled suddenly to face me. Her lovely features perplexed.

"Carl," she demanded worriedly, "aren't you well? You seem so strange. You act as if something has—"

I couldn't let her continue.

"I'm not going to work today," I told her. "I, I'm going to do some more work in my laboratory."

The girl called Gloria looked anxious.

"Not again, Carl," she protested. "They'll fire you one of these days if you continue to miss work."

I shrugged.

"It's little enough I'd lose." I felt safe in that statement.

"But, Carl," the girl protested again, "if you didn't spend such small fortunes on the equipment for your, your hobby laboratory in the basement, you'd be able to get along a little better on what you make!"

I shook my head.

"I'm not going to work today."

And then the girl quite unwittingly supplied the information I so desperately wanted.

"If they come here to see if you're really sick," she said, "and they find you in the basement downstairs working on chemical matters they weren't aware of, it will mean your job."

I put my hands on her shoulders as gently as I could.

"Don't worry, Gloria," I said. "I'm staying here today. It will be the last time I'll spend in the laboratory."

The girl gave me a peculiar glance.

"You said that last night," she declared. Then she was gone.

I looked at the key in my hand, and again the trip-hammer beating of my heart was dizzying with the dread excitement of the unknown...

TWENTY minutes later I had finished my search of the basement laboratory of Carl Gelsing.

The evidence I had found there served only to heap further coals upon the burning, maddening questions for which I sought answers.

There were papers, hundreds of them, in a large file. Newspaper clippings, magazine notations, book references, rotogravure pictures, everything and anything pertaining to the life, friends, habits and secrets of—*myself!*

I, Jonathan Lane, found an unimaginably detailed personal history of myself in those files. Found a history of myself painstakingly compiled by one Carl Gelsing, the man whose body I now possessed instead of my own.

What equipment of a scientific nature there had been in the laboratory was now totally destroyed. The basement room was a litter of shattered tubes, broken slides and demolished apparatus.

In one corner of the room there was a small mound of ashes, indicating that a small pile of papers had been touched to flame there and deliberately burned.

Aside from a tattered laboratory smock, there was little else. Nevertheless I searched on for another five minutes in the desperate hope that I might unearth something else that might give some faint clarity to this maddening puzzle.

Then, as I stood there bewilderedly, hopelessly, while the insanely impossible facts whirled around and around in my brain like some mad parody of reason, I was conscious of the first, hideously fantastic glimmering truth.

It was wild, impossible, the deduction of a mind at the brink of insanity. But it bore the grim plausibility of madness itself. I determined to see it through. It was the only action remaining to me...

IT took me a little more than an hour to get to my suburban mansion from the metropolitan slum section in which I'd found myself. And when at last I arrived at the sprawling, wide-lawned estate that had been mine less than twenty-four hours before, a feverish hysteria was again surging through me.

I stood there a moment at the big gates leading into the long gravel roadway, gazing wordlessly at the vast stone mansion set back among the trees. Stood there, while the hammering of my heart and the choking in my throat became almost more than I could stand.

Kermit admitted me, moments later, to the huge stone mansion. His tired old face was impassive as I told him I wanted to speak with Jonathan Lane.

For an instant, when my eyes had first met those of my old servant, I had been certain that he would recognize me, would somehow realize what had happened.

But there had been no glimmer of recognition in the old butler's appraising glance. He told me merely to wait in the reception room, while he saw if Mr. Lane desired to talk to me.

"And your name, sir?" Kermit asked.

I'd hesitated a moment. Hesitated, then said, "Carl Gelsing."

"Mr. Lane expects you, sir?" he inquired.

Again I hesitated.

"I think perhaps he does," I said. "And I feel certain the name will be familiar to him."

Kermit left me in the reception room. And when he reappeared again at last, he motioned toward the hallway leading to the study.

"Mr. Lane said for you to step into his study, sir. He'll be down in a moment."

There are no words to describe my emotions as I walked down that hallway to what had been my own study but hours before. No words quite apt enough to depict the sick excitement that flooded me as I took a chair in that study and waited for the entrance of the person who now owned my body.

Minutes passed, and the cold sweat on my forehead and half-terror in my heart grew stronger with every second of them. I tried to keep my eyes from straying to the old familiar objects around the room. The books I prized, the paintings, the curios on the desk.

And then I heard the voice—*my* voice, the voice belonging to the body of Jonathan Lane!

"Hello, Gelsing. I rather expected you'd come here."

I rose, wheeling, and faced the physical manifestation of what had been myself less than twenty-four hours ago. I stared open-mouthed wordlessly, as my body smiled tauntingly at me from the doorway.

"You are Gelsing," I managed at last. "You are Carl Gelsing. What horrible madness did you—"

GELSING, the man who had stolen my body and given me his, smiled again and waved his hand at my chair.

"Sit down," he said. "Sit down, and don't get excited. I'd hate to have you thrown out of here before we got a chance to talk this thing over."

Weakly, I slumped back into my chair, my eyes following him as he moved around behind the desk and sat down.

The silence hung heavily for a moment, while Gelsing, the man who now lived in my body, smiled appraisingly at me.

"You must have a very strong mind," he said at last, fingering a paper knife on the desk. "I had taken into consideration the possibility of your going mad on discovering what had happened to you." The smile became a smirk.

"You must be insane," I gasped.

He shook his head.

"Quite the contrary," he declared. He waved his hand to indicate the room.

"I am now one of the wealthiest young men in the nation," he said. "And with the wealth, which you never seemed to be able to utilize constructively, I will soon be one of the most powerful men in the world. No," he smirked, "I don't quite think I am insane."

"Then this was deliberately planned, devilishly exe—" I began.

He broke in again.

"It was quite cunningly planned," he said. "Undoubtedly you found the files on yourself in my laboratory. I began collecting them almost two years ago, when I realized that a discovery I had stumbled on would enable me to accomplish this some day.

"I chose your body, your wealth and station as the one I could best utilize," he went on. "From that day forward I obtained every last scrap of data about you, your history, your personal habits, friends, acquaintances, everything I could learn.

"And while I did so," he declared, "I continued to live in my miserable, poverty stricken surroundings, continued to slave night after night in that wretched basement laboratory, perfecting, testing, toiling over the power of mind—transference, which I had first discovered quite unwittingly. From the very moment that I made my selection, chose your body as the one which I would take over, the transformation you woke to find completed this morning was inevitable.

"Yes, indeed, you were an ideal choice for me. You were young, had enormous wealth, and exceedingly few domestic ties." He paused. "And now my initial plans are realized. The transference is made. I now have your body, and with it your life and fortune. You, my friend, have received in return my body, and the squalid life that goes with it."

"But you can't do this!" I protested. "You're mad. You don't know what you are doing!"

The smile left his face.

"Can't I?" he asked. "Or, shouldn't we say haven't I?"

"You have," I admitted thickly, desperately. "God knows you have, in some incredible fashion accomplished this impossible madness. But it can't go on. You must return both of us to where we belong!"

HE shrugged. "Even if I were fool enough to do so," he declared, "it would no longer be possible. You saw the smashed equipment in the basement laboratory. You viewed the ashes that remained of the formulae notations I worked from. I deliberately destroyed every last bridge back. There is no possibility of change any longer."

My mouth was open in horrified astonishment. Sickly, I tried to speak. Words refused to come from my lips. He grinned gloatingly at me.

"There is little need to be so alarmed," he declared. "There is no reason to feel that your life is at an end. Quite the contrary. A new, a very different life is just beginning for you." He laughed unpleasantly.

Still I fought for words.

He continued. "You'll find this new life very much in contrast to the one I've taken from you," he said. "Where once you had measureless wealth, you will now have grubbing poverty. Where once you knew nothing but luxury, now you will have little but toil and misery.

"But," he paused before going on, "there will be compensations." Scorn underlined the last word. "You will know the dubious thrill of struggle for existence. You will find that the lot of the little man, though not replete with comfort, has the compensation of dignity in poverty, honor in squalor. You will learn the beaten weariness of the man who fights against his fate. You will have despair, sorrow, bitter disappointment. And through it all your life will be one hell of a stark struggle to stay alive."

I watched him reach into a humidor at his elbow and bring forth one of the unusually expensive cigars I had smoked. His eyes regarding me behind the flame of the match for a moment of mocking derision, he lighted the cigar and spoke again.

"But you will have love," he said, and the scornful mockery in his voice was even stronger now.

"That girl," I found myself saying, scarcely aware that speech had returned, "that girl who knocked at your door this morning. You—"

He cut me off.

"She is very much in love with me," he said smirkingly, "or with what once was me. She is part of the sublime and simple life I leave to you. She need never know. I want no more of her. She's part of the nightmare of squalor and poverty that I've forever left behind me."

I thought of her sweet warm lips, the perfume from her lovely ebon hair, the adoration shining from her eyes in that worn snapshot I'd found in the wallet.

"You swine!" I said hoarsely. "You mad, rotten swine!"

His face went suddenly white in instant rage.

"Hold your tongue, *Gelsing!*" he snapped. "Hold your tongue or I'll have you tossed out of here instantly!"

I WAS thinking, still, of the girl, Gloria. I was thinking of her words when, unknowing, she had looked, at me that morning, saying, *"You acted as if, as if you'd never see me again."* I was thinking of the tears in her lovely eyes as she said those words.

Suddenly I rose, taking a step toward the desk where my usurper sat. He rose, too, wrathfully.

"Stay where you are!" he cried. "Don't move a step closer!"

I shook my head.

"I've no intention of harming you," I told him. "As a matter of fact, I'm just leaving. I'm going back to the life you gave me. I'm returning to the love of the beautiful girl you gave me. I'm going to take my chances at carving a new destiny out of the clay you've given me. I think it will be more than worth the battle. I think perhaps I will enjoy it."

The rage was still stamped whitely on his face.

"That's fine," he grated. "Now get the hell out of here."

Quite suddenly, then, the white wrath on his face went sickly yellow. He clutched at his heart, his breathing suddenly gasping, loud. He reeled and swayed on his feet.

"You'd better sit down," I told him quietly. "You'd better learn not to excite yourself during the next three months. You see, there's something about me that you didn't find out, something I myself learned only three weeks ago."

Sweat was on his brow as he slumped to the chair behind the desk. A latent fear was growing in his eyes.

"What do you mean?" he gasped. "For God's sake, what do you mean?"

I smiled then.

"You see, three weeks ago my physician advised me that I had but four months more, at the utmost, to live. He told me that there was absolutely nothing in medical science that my money could buy to save me."

I turned then, moving to the door of the study. There I paused an instant.

"I came here hoping to save you from your folly. But, as you pointed out, that is no longer possible. Goodbye, Jonathan Lane. May your last three months be pleasant ones."

## THE END

# Ricardo's Virus

## By WILLIAM TENN

*A knife wound can be a serious matter on Earth. On Venus, it's a six-hour flow into vilest eternity.*

GRAFF DINGLE stolidly watched yellow mold form around the stiletto hole in his arm. He smelled the first faint jasmine odor of the disease and glanced up to where the sun glowed unhappily behind a mass of dirty clouds and wind-driven rain.

Dingle kicked morosely at the Heatwave thug left behind to ambush him, and the charred body turned soughingly in the mud. "Be seeing you, bully-boy, in about five and a half hours. Your electroblast may have missed me, but it cooked my antiseptic pouch into soup. It made that last knife-thrust really rate."

There was a dumb dryhorn blunder, Graff reflected, sneering at himself out of a face that was dark from life-long exposure to a huge sun. Bending over an enemy before making certain he was burned to a crisp.

But he'd had to search the man's clothing for a clue to the disappearance of Greta and Dr. Bergenson and—even above Greta—the unspeakably precious cargo of lobodin they'd been flying in from Earth.

*So I'll pay for my hurry,* he thought. *Like one always does in the Venusian jungle.*

Ricardo's Virus was viciously prompt: six hours after its light, saffron globules had formed in an open wound and you were dead. And no frantic surgery, no pathetic attempts at drainage, could save you. Graff should know. His parents, his brothers and sisters had been a small fraction of the New Kalamazoo death totals due to cuts and scratches observed too late for antisepsis. The virus had accounted for most of three generations of Venusian colonists, including Vilfredo Ricardo himself, the first man to set hesitant foot on the swampy planet. Ricardo had merely skinned his hand on his new flagpole.

Nasty to die of the filthy mold before he knew what had happened to the Bergensons. Not that he had a personal interest in the matter any more for Greta wouldn't be marrying a corpse when she could pick any one of a hundred extremely live and woman-hungry pioneers. But her father was the only doctor in the tiny settlement. And the loss of the lobodin meant Ricardo's Virus would tuck many more New Kalamazoo colonists into seepy graves before the year was out.

A speck grew large in the sky. Graff involuntarily moved into the shade of a giant rosebush as his over sharp instincts asserted themselves.

Yes, it was a terry all right. Friendly?

THE pterodactyl landed lightly on a frond of the opposite fern. Its absurd, leathery forehead wrinkled at him. Graff noted that it was barely out of range of his electroblast. Intelligent, sure enough, and an unusually fearless specimen to perch this close to man.

At any other time he would have been intrigued by the opportunity of making friends with one of the intelligent winged reptiles who had learned to speak man's languages and, with good reason, shun his works. Now, he had other things on his mind.

Like dying painfully in a few hours.

Graff looked up sharply as enormous bat-like wings ceased their rustle.

The lizard-bird's long, sloping forehead wrinkled even further. Its beak opened and closed several times. It cleared its throat.

"City?"

Then it was civilized, too. What had induced it to leave its communal eyrie in the San Mountains? The terries had avoided men for over fifty years. Many was the time that Graff, intent on stalking meat for the colonists, had been startled by a flock of pterodactyls winging overhead and shouting curses down at him in the three languages of the early settlers.

"City?" the question was repeated more insistently. "Heatwave or New Kalamazoo?"

"New Kalamazoo."

A relieved nod of the triangular head. "This I thought. You wish knowledge which Heatwave man has man and girl from shif?"

Graff's whole body tensed. "Yes! Do you know?"

Another nod. "This I know. Name is Fuvina."

"Fuvina?" The hunter repeated it with a frown. He knew the names of most of Heatwave's big shots; some were political criminals, escaped from Earth. Others were former residents of his own town who had left in search of an easier living than the continual struggle with marshy soil and carnivorous jungle.

But he couldn't recall any Fuvina. Possibly a new arrival; possibly one of the smaller fry who had recently killed and looted his way to the top of bloody Heatwave society. Fuvina? Fuv—

Of course! The not-quite-flexible pterodactyl beak was incapable of labial sounds like *p* and *b,* and transformed them into the labiodentals *f* and *v.* Pubina! Max Pubina had left New Kalamazoo in a hurry three years ago after cutting some farmer's throat in a boundary dispute and, by combining organized raids on isolated families with the smuggling of the illicit Venusian dunging drug to Earth, had become a power of sorts.

"You mean Pubina?"

"This I said. Fuvina. He and other Heatwave men took man and girl from shif and placed them in own shif. Also took vig green vottle. Left one Heatwave man hidden here. Then flew that way in own shif. A fantastically large and fleshy wing gestured south. "Them I follow. Where Heatwave men stof, I see. Then I come vack."

The terry drew an immense swallow of air to compensate for his long speech and shook himself. The great fern trembled in sympathy.

GRAFF stepped forward from the rosebush and inspected his informant closely. "Thanks. But I don't see why you're interested."

The toothed beak, which was half as long as a man, opened uncertainly. "Vecause," the lizard-bird explained in a low voice, "Heatwave men have caftured my mate vefore attacking New Kalamazoo skyshif. In cage they fut her for shivment to Earth. This I can do nothing about fy myself. Vut them I follow, hofing to find way to rescue her."

"And you figure that if you help me find my friends, I'll help you save your mate from the sideshows on Earth? Well, I will, *if*—"

A big, complex *if,* with as many tendrils as sucking ivy. If he lived long enough, and, if he did, if he would be sane enough—considering the agonizing last hour of Ricardo's Virus infection—to do anything constructive once he arrived at Pubina's jungle hideout. If a man, guided by a pterodactyl flying overhead, could pick his way on foot through a completely unexplored section of swamp and have enough juice left in him when he emerged to take the prize of the century away from the toughest collection of cutthroats on an extremely tough planet.

He clenched his fist as the cramps began in his left hand—the cramps that would spread slowly throughout his body until they ended in fatal convulsions some five hours from now. If a one-armed man could do all this, and do it with just one portable electroblast...

He cursed sharply, suddenly, as he realized he'd been holding the electroblast in his hand ever since he'd given the Heatwave thug that finishing jolt. That was after he'd been stabbed, after the man's first wild blast had burned Graff's antiseptic pouch into a mess of fused glass vials and blackened fabric. Without immediate application of the ten different antiseptic solutions.

But now! He inspected the bright metal of the coils anxiously. Might still do. Just might. He holstered the blaster with infinite tenderness and stooped over the blackened body that had almost disappeared into the mud. The man's electric gun was far too wet to be of any use but Graff fumbled around in the soggy soil until he located the stiletto.

He straightened and grinned at the long blade, its steel already reddening from the pervasive rust of Venus.

"Where is the ship?" he asked. "The ship my friends were in?"

The terry nodded at a flat and soggy expanse. "Under there. Heatwave skyshif wait here high uf. When New Kalamazoo shif come, Heatwave shif fly down fast ufon it. New Kalamazoo shif hit mud hard. This I see. Then Heatwave men take your friends away and New Kalamazoo shif sink in mud. Altogether are four Heatwave men, vesides Fuvina. You kill one, so now are only three, vesides Fuvina." The flying reptile breathed heavily again. Its scaly claws moved restlessly about on the branch.

*Call that a break,* Graff decided. Four men to handle. Might have been twenty. Either Pubina had a smaller gang than had been believed, or he was playing the whole thing really smart. Toughs, especially Venusian ones, would really chop each other to merry hell over the first laboratory sample of a vaccine that promised immunity from Ricardo's Virus. A break to balance the loss of the ship.

Or was it? All he had was the terry's word. Could be that the entire yarn about his mate being captured for export to the Terran amusement parks was nothing more than a story made up by Pubina to play on a colonist's sympathy. The terry might be working for Pubina some way or other. Who knew anything about pterodactyls? Who knew if they experienced anything like love or loyalty?

Graff stared at the unwinking reptilian eyes, at the tapering ugly beak, both completely devoid of expression. Add another *if.*

"All right, MacDuff," he said at last. "Lead on."

"We go in vig curve," the terry told him, flapping its wings monstrously in preparation for flight. "Eight, nine hours for you. Other way take half time, vut—"

"Vut nothing," Graff broke in. He massaged his left forearm, which had begun aching in sympathy with the hand. "Let's use the short cut."

"It too hard for you, too dangerous! River cuts across—"

"So—I'll get my feet wet. I'm not in a position to be worried by pneumonia. Let's head for the straight and narrow, MacDuff. I'm in a hurry."

THE animal cocked its head to one side, dropped its wings in a gesture like a shrug and moved off the fern in a soaring glide southward. When it was about three hundred feet up, it circled back to make certain that Graff was following.

Now if you ever go to Venus, the Polar Continent is probably where you'll live for the duration of your stay. Not only is its temperature and annual rainfall the lowest on the planet (which makes it just a shade more uncomfortable than the Amazonian Jungle), but also it is the most heavily populated stretch of land—averaging close to one person every thirty square miles.

But if you find yourself on the Polar Continent you will be advised, and well advised, to stay away from the Southern Peninsula. This is not merely because it is a dank and deadly swamp. But chiefly because of the Black River, which winds through the peninsula, doubling back on itself, crossing through itself and becoming a tributary of itself a dozen times over, like a living surrealist corkscrew.

The Black River rises somewhere in the unscalable peaks of the San Mountains and comes roaring into the flatlands with a tremendous velocity. Just before reaching the peninsula, however, it is joined by the Zetzot River, and the two of them make a combination that is really in a hurry. Even if there were no rain at all (which is definitely not the case) there would be a perpetual mist over the Southern Peninsula. And by the time the Black gets through doubling back on itself, giving itself a shove, so to speak—well, the reason no one knows exactly where the river empties into the Jefferson Sea is because the entire area is completely obscured by an opaque steaming fog, which boils about for miles on either side.

Nor is that all. Certain animals like to wallow in the swamp created by the Black. And most of them are very large. Creatures that can survive in the swamp of the Southern Peninsula are quite tough, quite dangerous and most uniquely suited to their environment. There are snakes and insects and carnivorous plants galore, not to mention the huge creatures who live in quicksand and have yet to be classified. One of the smallest animals of the peninsula is a dark little fish, which swims back and forth in the Black itself. Venusian colonists have christened it the sardine, possibly because it is the size of a terrestrial sardine. Its habits, however, resemble those of the South American piranha. It travels in large schools and eats its way through anything.

All in all, the Southern Peninsular Swamp is an ideal home for a baron of crime who wants to get away from it all. The *all* doesn't include law, of course. On Venus, each man writes his own code of laws with the weapon he finds handiest.

The trouble was, Graff Dingle reflected, as he found a ford and leaped across the screaming waters to the opposite bank, the trouble was that his folks and people like them had come to Venus to get away from lawlessness of the international kind only to hit the inevitable individual lawlessness of a frontier.

Ordinarily a frontier is slowly and surely transformed from rowdy wide-openness into suburban quietude by the increase in population—but population doesn't increase in really dangerous spots; that's why the people of New Kalamazoo worked so hard and so long to make their settlement large enough to merit the establishment of a university. A university would mean laboratories and research facilities to investigate Ricardo's Virus and all the lesser plagues peculiar to Venus, the plagues, which took more lives yearly than jungle monsters and murderous Heatwavers combined, and a university would mean an increase in population, and law and order.

But Earth hadn't been interested. The study of Venusian diseases was an exotic subject hardly touched upon in Terran medical schools. Earth had been far too busy manufacturing artificial diseases to supplement atom bombs and hydrogen bombs.

Earth had, however, investigated the Venusian plagues with a view to their use in biological warfare. And out of the investigation, as an accident, as a by-product, had come lobodin. A vaccine, not a serum. No good for Graff right now, for he was almost two full hours into the yellow death.

HE WORKED his left arm around slowly, wincing with each turn, his eyes on the terry above him circling southward in the damp murky sky. At the same time he tried to plant the broad soles of his boots on mud that wasn't quicksand, on rotten twigs that wouldn't crack too loudly. He knew his blood was now completely infiltrated with the obscene little yellow specks.

Pubina was probably trying to force Dr. Bergenson to inject the vaccine into him, ridiculing the old man's protests that all the bottle held was a starter culture, just enough so that with weeks of careful tending they might have sufficient vaccine to immunize the children.

It had been so expensive and difficult for the little colony to send Dr. Bergenson and Greta to Earth where his reputation and connections had enabled him to wheedle a spoonful of the precious stuff out of a government laboratory... Pubina hadn't been able to get it, for all of his bribes and underworld contacts. But the bribes and underworld contacts had served another purpose: Pubina had discovered when the Bergensons were due to return—and that was all he really needed.

Graff noticed abruptly that the terry was falling rapidly back at him. Could he be trying to warn—

A shriek gave him the answer. Less than a quarter-mile away, a brontosaurus squatted its tremendous bulk in a shallow pool and regarded him from the end of an undulating snake-like neck. The animal screamed again and Graff froze.

He watched the incredibly heavy reptile scramble to its feet and desperately tried to think. It wasn't a brontosaurus charge you had to be afraid of, but what usually traveled in its wake. A brontosaurus was herbivorous and, for all its size, extremely timid. It was ridiculous, possibly, but the mountain of living flesh was probably screaming in terror at the sight of him. You only had to control yourself and think while the great beast charged…because a brontosaurus meets danger by running into it.

It is so massive that it is virtually unstoppable once in motion. You can blast its stupid little head off and it will keep running for another twenty minutes, powered by the bundle of nerve cells just under the spine. You just have to stand still and remember that it is much more frightened than you and is trying to trample you to death before you can bite it.

Graff stood his ground, bending his knees slowly, until the behemoth was only twenty-five feet away. Then he straightened suddenly and leaped off to the right, then again, further, and again, still further to the right.

SCREAMING insanely, the tons upon tons of flesh roared past, absolutely unable to halt itself. Its momentum carried it up a small hill and Graff could hear it bellowing down the other side. It wouldn't return.

But something else was on its way. There's always a meat-eater in the wake of a brontosaurus. Sometimes there are several. The *kind* of carnivore was very important to Graff right now. He had an electroblast, which he wasn't certain would work in an emergency, whose diminished power he'd certainly need later. And he had a stiletto.

He heard the beast thumping its way through the luxuriant weeds of the swamp. A moment later it had broken into the clear, had seen him and was loping toward him easily with all the confidence of a powerful creature that sees an easy meal in sight.

A shata. No larger than a terran wolf. But if a brontosaurus can be said to be all body-bulk and very little head, the shata is just the reverse. Twelve rows of teeth, and jaws, which open wide enough to admit a sheep. Regretfully and a little uncertainly, Graff holstered the electroblast and balanced the stiletto on his palm. He'd hunted lots of shata in his time, but never with a knife.

He began weaving about, conscious of his awkwardness. The knots in his left side constantly made him misjudge his body and slip off balance. And here he was hoping to take four men at a time—

As he expected, the shata was confused by his peculiar motion. It slowed to a dead stop, then slunk before him, growling. It moved in half-circles, coming in closer each time. Graff waited until it was directly in front of him. He stood still and immediately the shata sprang, jaws gaping.

The palate. Just behind the palate is the brain. It means sticking half your arm into a fearful set of jaws, but do it right…

Graff let the rigid, distended head slide off the knife and into the mud. He wiped his blade on the green fur, standing out like so many spikes, and grimaced. A nice specimen. Shatas were good eating, too.

Well, he wasn't a hunter any more. He was a dead man looking for a coffin. He was swamp-bait if he collapsed in this weedy muck.

The terry skimmed by with his head turned questioningly.

"I'm fine," Graff reassured him. "How much farther?"

"Vetween one and two of your hours." The lizard-bird curved up and ahead, leathery wings beating slowly.

Graff plodded on. He should arrive with about an hour and a half of life left. That would give him a half-hour to an hour at most in which to operate consciously and more or less effectively. After that there would be half an hour of writhing agony, leading into unconsciousness. After that he would be dead.

He'd hate to leave life. It meant leaving the thrill of tracking your quarry on the bracing slope of Mount Catiline where the dodle breeds in the Season of Wind-Driven Rains; it meant leaving a wild new world that was just a-borning as far as humanity was concerned; it meant leaving Greta Bergenson.

It also meant leaving wealth. Now that lobodin had been developed, the colonization of Venus would begin in earnest. He was the last alive of a numerous family who had homesteaded half the Galertan Archipelago into their possession. He was heir to all the rich, fertile and deserted islands his father and brothers had claimed. With Ricardo's Virus taken care of, future Venusian farmers would pay well for those scattered spots of soil in the Jefferson Sea.

Following the terry, he hit the river again. He started downstream, looking for a ford as he had before. The Black was rather wide at this point and he wasted fifteen precious minutes before he found a bank that curved near enough to the opposite one to permit of a leap. He went into the weeds to get a running start.

A shadow plummeted past him.

"Vack," the terry screamed. "Get vack! Don't jumf here. Gridnik!"

Graff paused and peered across the river. Sure enough, there was the brown and white nest on the opposite bank where he would have landed. As he watched, a single gridnik droned out, looking like a winged red ant but with the size and disposition of a large, cornered rat.

"Thanks, MacDuff," he muttered, moving away. Well, there was no help for it. He didn't have time to look for another ford. He'd have to swim.

He waited on the crumbling bank until a dozen blue flashes swept past under him. "Sardine" schools were usually far enough apart to permit a fast swimmer to get through between them. When the tiny blue fish were fifty feet away, he dived.

The force of the river knocked the breath out of him. He fought his way through the torrent. His flailing hands touched a projecting piece of rock and he hauled himself painfully up the bank.

Graff noted gratefully that his head was clearer. The gnawing headache had diminished somewhat under the impact of the water.

The pterodactyl alighted near him. "There," it said, pointing ahead with a yellow claw. "Fuvina."

But the hunter was interested in something else. He removed his electroblast and examined its coils ruefully. The tight holster was supposed to be fairly waterproof, but it had not been intended for protecting a weapon in the Black River.

He started to throw it aside, but held it as he remembered how few cards he held in his hand.

MAX PUBINA'S hideout was a large prefabricated job that must have cost a medium-sized fortune to import from Earth across some thirty million miles of empty space. The outlaw's house covered the top of a rise, and the soil around it was sufficiently high over the swamp proper to resemble the fine farmland of New Kalamazoo. Rich jungle growths were held at bay by a patch of sandy ground completely surrounding the house. It made it impossible for anyone or anything to creep up to the walls unobserved. Graff Dingle knew how expensive it must have been to sterilize so large an area of ground.

*Crime does not pay,* he mused. *Except on Venus.*

He reconnoitered the place cautiously, keeping well under cover. The man-made yard was empty. There was no one outside the house or the rocket ship hangar attached to it. He could see the blunt nose of Pubina's sleek craft in the otherwise deserted hangar. But they probably had guards posted at the windows.

A long white line traced a curve in his path. Graff stepped over it gingerly, glancing to the left. Sure enough, hidden in thick bushes was the mass of white filaments that was the bulk of the sucking ivy. Touch the trigger-vine, however gently with your foot...

He came back to the terry. "Listen, MacDuff," he said. "I want you to stay out of trouble as long as possible. When I need you, I'll need you bad. Meanwhile, on the wing or on the ground, you're a sucker for an electroblast with that wingspread. But you could be useful as a lookout. I wouldn't like to be outflanked."

A grave nod of the narrow beak. "This I do." The reptile soared up in a high spiral over the house.

Now. He had to get into the house across thirty-five feet of open ground, under the electroblasts of four highly proficient murderers. How?

The headache returned, stronger than ever, and Graff swayed dizzily. Red roaring fires tore up and down his left side. He'd never make it. Swamp-bait, that's all he was, bait for the mud of the Black.

He straightened then and laughed. Bait? Well, that was one way to hunt.

The hunter strode toward the house, across the creeper of sucking ivy, counting each step. He stopped under cover of a sweeping fern just outside the sandy expanse.

"Pubina!" he yelled. "I've come for the Bergensons."

There was a flicker at one of the windows. "Who are you?"

"Graff Dingle of New Kalamazoo. Listen, Pubina, I'll trade the rest of our lobodin for Greta Bergenson and her father."

A pause while they digested this. Then: "Send one of your men in and we'll talk it over, Dingle."

"Can't. I'm alone. Send one of your men out with the Bergensons, and I'll give you the lobodin."

No reason for Pubina to be certain that the Bergenson lobodin represented the first and only shipment. And what he claimed to have would raise the quantity to the point where all of the outlaws could be vaccinated.

The terry came down behind him and whispered gently, "Three men leave house from rear. Two coming around on left, one on right.  Man on right has clearer fath, so will ve here first."

Graff gestured assent with the electroblast.  He heard the terry take off again.

Pubina was being safe and cozy.  Sending his henchmen while he held the fort himself.

He heard a soggy clump to the right and grinned.  Why, the man was making more noise than a dryhorn freshly arrived from Terra!  When he saw the black waterproof jumper through the high weeds, he stepped out from under the fern and moved backwards.  He held the electroblast out, as if it worked.

The outlaw's face, lined with years of dunging inhalation, broke into a lunatic smile.  Since Graff wasn't looking at him, he deduced Graff hadn't seen him.  Pubina's henchman took larger steps.  Graff backed.

He counted as he retreated.  He counted slowly, taking steps that were uniform and even, looking off to the side of the outlaw, trying to keep his tortured body from making a deadly mis-step.

There!  He breathed gustily as he saw he'd passed the white line.  The outlaw crept forward, crouching, trying to get close enough for a certain blast.  He too noticed the trigger vine, and stepped daintily across it.

Graff whirled to face him then, electroblast at the ready.  The man jumped—and one boot dug into the creeper!

He barely had time to scream.  A haze of white tendrils whipped around him, each armed with thousands of microscopic suckers.  A moment later the bloodless husk that had been a human was being dropped from the sucking ivy's clutches, rattling like so much paper.

The scream had been heard.  Graff's jungle-trained ears caught the whispers of the other two men on his left as they conferred worriedly.  If only he had a decent weapon.  Anything besides the stiletto.  He could take such dryhorns with an old-fashioned pistol!

But he didn't have a pistol. All he had was twenty-seven years' experience on Venus as a native-born citizen. So he began to run.

He stopped after a moment and listened. The crashes behind him indicated he was being pursued. If he was afraid, the outlaws had evidently decided, he was weak enough to chase. Graff ran toward the Tuscany.

By the time he reached the river, he was weaving from side to side and sobbing. The exertion magnified his pain a thousand-fold. His pursuers were getting closer. Desperately, he trotted downstream.

They were quite close now. He heard them chuckling and calling to each other triumphantly—but there was the Gridnik nest!

He waited just a moment, poised on the bank of the river, until they broke into the clear, almost within electroblast range. Then, as they caught sight of him and increased their speed, he hurled his useless weapon into the striped little dome—and jumped.

WHEN he came threshing out of the water, twenty feet further down the bank, the hideous swarm of insects were still gorging themselves. Graff crept away, nauseated. He rubbed his eyes against the darkness welling within them.

"MacDuff!" he called, his voice crackling with agony. "MacDuff!"

The terry swept down to his side.

"Listen, pal, I haven't got much time left, so we'll have to hurry. No more fancy stuff. Think you can fly in the rear windows or something, by way of diversion? It'll give me time to cross the sandy stretch."

Without a word, the lizard-bird went away. Graff came to the edge of the arid soil surrounding the pre-fab and waited.

He saw the enormous shadow tilt down behind the house and heard the crash of breaking glass. He threw himself forward. Sand boiled away from his boots. His head wobbled as if his neck had ceased to exist. Must be getting close to deadline time, Graff decided. A few minutes more at most before he caved in completely. He drew the stiletto out, holding it with difficulty in a twitching hand.

There was a yell inside the house and the sizzle of an electroblast bolt. As he smashed into the door, he heard the electroblast go off again.

He saw a huge cage holding a fluttering pterodactyl as he tottered into the living room. Dr. Bergenson and Greta were tied to chairs with long coils of fongool vine. Greta's pink overall-jumper was ripped and there was the mark of a man's hand on her face. Pubina stood under a charred hole in the ceiling where his first blast had gone wild. At his feet, a hole neatly burned in one wing, writhed MacDuff, awaiting the finisher.

Pubina whirled to face Graff, his electroblast coming up swiftly. The hunter staggered toward him, fully conscious of his lack of speed, his almost infantile weakness. Knots of pain pulled at his knees.

The Heatwaver's forefinger flicked down on the firing button. MacDuff lifted himself on his one good wing and lunged at the boot before him. His long beak closed on Pubina's ankle. There was a horrible bony crunch and the outlaw cursed, turning to beat down at the reptile.

Graff reached them, almost falling against Pubina. For a moment he couldn't coordinate his arm muscles enough to use the stiletto; then, sinking his teeth deep into his own lip, he drove the thin blade ahead. Pubina shrieked and fell, the stiletto throbbing in his side.

Deciding to let MacDuff finish him, even if the terry was making a mess of it, Graff bent over clumsily and retrieved the electroblast Pubina had dropped. He almost went over backwards as he straightened.

Placing one foot in front of the other intently, he walked to the Bergensons. He slid like a man walking on banana skins.

Darkness roiled all about him now and every cell in his body seemed to writhe.

The bottle containing the vaccine was on a table, he noticed. It was still full; the shining hypodermic beside it was empty. Good.

Very carefully, he burned off the fongool vine with the electroblast at low power. Greta rushed toward him, but he slipped and fell at her feet.

"Darling," he heard her sob; it sounded as if her voice were on the other side of the Jefferson Sea. "You're infected! Oh, Graff, Graff! The lobodin won't work on an infected case!"

"I know," he muttered thickly, and let his head loll round to where the terry was inching along the floor to the cage in the corner. The last thing he saw was the neat little hole in the wing.

"Be seeing you, MacDuff," Graff whispered as the darkness came down, pinpointed with multitudes of exploding yellow dots...

That was why he was so surprised when he opened his eyes to see the terry perched by his bed with a neat patch of gauze taped to one wing.

"How in hell did you pull through, MacDuff?" he asked.

"The same way as you," the lizard-bird told him. "We are voth natives of Venus."

"Huh?" He raised himself waveringly on one elbow. He was lying in the Bergenson home in New Kalamazoo. They must have used Pubina's rocket ship to fly back. "What do you mean—*native?*"

"Just what he says, Graff." Greta pushed open the screen door and bustled in with a pile of linen. "You were both born on Venus. Father says that you must have had all kinds of skin abrasions as an infant: your body developed a natural immunity to Ricardo's Virus. We'll still use the vaccine on everybody else, including the children, just to be on the safe side. But Father has felt for a long time that the blood of the pioneers would adjust to its environment. When you got sick, but didn't die, you proved it."

"Well, I'd like to point out," Graff said, as he sat up to permit Greta to change his sheets, "that I am very, very happy to have given your father a chance to prove that theory."

MacDuff closed a lidless eye in an assenting reptilian wink.

## THE END

# Mariana

## By FRITZ LEIBER

*Jonathan told her not to touch the switches, but it was cold and lonely and isolated...*

MARIANA had been living in the big villa and hating the tall pine trees around it for what seemed like an eternity when she found the secret panel in the master control panel of the house.

The secret panel was simply a narrow blank of aluminum—she'd thought of it as room for more switches if they ever needed any, perish the thought!—between the air-conditioning controls and the gravity controls. Above the switches for the three-dimensional TV but below those for the robot butler and maids.

Jonathan had told her not to fool with the master control panel while he was in the city, because she would wreck anything electrical, so when the secret panel came loose under her aimlessly questing fingers and fell to the solid rock floor of the patio with a musical *twing* her first reaction was fear.

Then she saw it was only a small blank oblong of sheet aluminum that had fallen and that in the space it had covered was a column of six little switches. Only the top one was identified. Tiny glowing letters beside it spelled TREES and it was on.

When Jonathan got home from the city that evening she gathered her courage and told him about it. He was neither particularly angry nor impressed.

"Of course there's a switch for the trees," he informed her deflatingly, motioning the robot butler to cut his steak. "Didn't you know they were radio trees? I didn't want to wait 25 years for them and they couldn't grow in this rock anyway. A station in the city broadcasts a master pine tree and sets like ours pick it up and project it around homes. It's vulgar but convenient."

After a bit she asked timidly, "Jonathan, are the radio pine trees ghostly as you drive through them?"

"Of course not! They're solid as this house and the rock under it—to the eye and to the touch too. If you ever stirred outside you'd know these things. The city station transmits pulses of matter at 60 cycles a second like alternating current. The science of it is over your head."

She ventured one more question: "Why did they have the tree switch covered up?"

"So you wouldn't monkey with it—same as the fine controls on the TV. And so you wouldn't get ideas and start changing the trees. It would unsettle *me,* let me tell you, to come home to oaks one day and birches the next. I like consistency and I like pines." He looked at them out of the dining room picture window and grunted with satisfaction.

She had been meaning to tell him about hating the pines, but that discouraged her and she dropped the topic.

About noon the next day, however, she went to the secret panel and switched off the pine trees and quickly turned around to watch them.

At first nothing happened and she was beginning to think that Jonathan was wrong again, as he so often was though would never admit, but then they began to waver and specks of pale green light churned across them and then they faded and were gone, leaving behind only an intolerably bright single point of light—just as when the TV is switched off. The star hovered motionless for what seemed a long time, then backed away and raced off toward the horizon.

Now that the pine trees were out of the way Mariana could see the real landscape. It was flat gray rock, endless miles of it, exactly the same as the rock on which the house was set and which formed the floor of the patio. It was the same in every direction. One black two-lane road drove straight across it—nothing more.

She disliked the view almost at once—it was dreadfully lonely and depressing. She switched the gravity to moon-normal and danced about dreamily, floating over the middle-of-the-room bookshelves and the grand piano and even having the robot maids dance with her, but it did not cheer her. About two o'clock she went to switch on the pine trees again, as she had intended to do in any case before Jonathan came home and was furious.

However, she found there had been changes in the column of six little switches. The TREES switch no longer had its glowing name. She remembered that it had been the top one, but the top one would not turn on again. She tried to force it from "off" to "on" but it would not move.

All the rest of the afternoon she sat on the steps outside the front door watching the black two-lane road. Never a car or a person came into view until Jonathan's tan roadster appeared, seeming at first to hang motionless in the distance and then to move only like a microscopic snail although she knew he always drove at top speed—it was one of the reasons she would never get in the car with him.

Jonathan was not as furious as she had feared. "Your own damn fault for meddling with it," he said curtly. "Now we'll have to get a man out here. Dammit, I hate to eat supper looking at nothing but those rocks! Bad enough driving through them twice a day."

She asked him haltingly about the barrenness of the landscape and the absence of neighbors.

"Well, you wanted to live *way out*," he told her. "You wouldn't ever have known about it if you hadn't turned off the trees."

"There's one other thing I've got to bother you with, Jonathan," she said. "Now the second switch—the one next below—has got a name that glows. It just says HOUSE. It's turned on—I haven't touched it! Do you suppose…"

"I want to look at this," he said, bounding up from the couch and slamming his martini-on-the-rocks tumbler down on the tray of the robot maid so that she rattled. "I bought this house as solid, but there are swindles. Ordinarily I'd spot a broadcast style in a flash, but they just might have slipped me a job relayed from some other planet or solar system. Fine thing if me and fifty other multi-megabuck men were spotted around in identical houses, each thinking his was unique."

"But if the house is based on rock like it is…"

"That would just make it easier for them to pull the trick, you dumb bunny!"

They reached the master control panel. "There it is," she said helpfully, jabbing out a finger…and hit the HOUSE switch.

For a moment nothing happened, then a white churning ran across the ceiling, the walls and furniture started to swell and bubble like cold lava, and then they were alone on a rock table big as three tennis courts. Even the master control panel was gone. The only thing that was left was a slender rod coming out of the gray stone at their feet and bearing at the top, like some mechanistic fruit, a small block with the six switches—that and an intolerably bright star hanging in the air where the master bedroom had been.

Mariana pushed frantically at the HOUSE switch, but it was unlabeled now and locked in the "off" position, although she threw her weight at it stiff-armed.

The upstairs star sped off like an incendiary bullet, but its last flashbulb glare showed her Jonathan's face set in lines of fury. He lifted his hands like talons.

"You little idiot!" he screamed, coming at her.

"No, Jonathan, no!" she wailed, backing off, but he kept coming.

She realized that the block of switches had broken off in her hands. The third switch had a glowing name now: JONATHAN. She flipped it.

As his fingers dug into her bare shoulders they seemed to turn to foam rubber, then to air. His face and gray flannel suit seethed iridescently, like a leprous ghost's, then melted and ran. His star, smaller than that of the house but much closer, seared her eyes. When she opened them again there was nothing at all left of the star or Jonathan but a dancing dark afterimage like a black tennis ball.

She was alone on an infinite flat rock plain under the cloudless, star-specked sky.

The fourth switch had its glowing name now: STARS.

It was almost dawn by her radium-dialed wristwatch and she was thoroughly chilled, when she finally decided to switch off the stars. She did not want to do it—in their slow wheeling across the sky they were the last sign of orderly reality—but it seemed the only move she could make.

She wondered what the fifth switch would say. ROCKS? AIR? Or even...?

She switched off the stars.

The Milky Way, arching in all its unalterable glory, began to churn, its component stars darting about like midges. Soon only one remained, brighter even than Sirius or Venus—until it jerked back, fading, and darted to infinity.

The fifth switch said DOCTOR and it was not on but off.

An inexplicable terror welled up in Mariana. She did not even want to touch the fifth switch. She set the block of switches down on the rock and backed away from it.

But she dared not go far in the starless dark. She huddled down and waited for dawn. From time to time she looked at her watch dial and at the night-light glow of the switch-label a dozen yards away.

It seemed to be growing much colder.

She read her watch dial. It was two hours past sunrise. She remembered they had taught her in third grade that the sun was just one more star.

She went back and sat down beside the block of switches and picked it up with a shudder and flipped the fifth switch.

The rock grew soft and crisply fragrant under her and lapped up over her legs and then slowly turned white.

She was sitting in a hospital bed in a small blue room with a white pinstripe.

A sweet, mechanical voice came out of the wall, saying, "You have interrupted the wish-fulfillment therapy by your own decision. If you now recognize your sick depression and are willing to accept help, the doctor will come to you. If not, you are at liberty to return to the wish-fulfillment therapy and pursue it to its ultimate conclusion."

Mariana looked down. She still had the block of switches in her hands and the fifth switch still read DOCTOR.

The wall said, "I assume from your silence that you will accept treatment. The doctor will be with you immediately."

The inexplicable terror returned to Mariana with compulsive intensity.

She switched off the doctor.

She was back in the starless dark. The rocks had grown very much colder. She could feel icy feathers falling on her face— snow.

She lifted the block of switches and saw, to her unutterable relief that the sixth and last switch now read, in tiny glowing letters: MARIANA.

## THE END

# Saucer! Saucer!

## By HENRY SLESAR

*This flying saucer business has got everybody all mixed up. You keep hearing about sightings and meeting people who had a friend who knew a guy who saw one. But how do you start investigating on your own? Well, why not follow Bill Dover's hunch? He started looking in a mental institution.*

WILLIAM DOVER was a columnist for a small news service operating out of Cincinnati, Ohio. He was an eager young man with a sharp, alert face, and a reputation for quick thinking. He had only one outstanding fault. He believed in Flying Saucers.

It was only natural, then, that Bill Dover should get excited when a Saucer story developed virtually in his own backyard. The place was Hillsboro, Tennessee, only a short hop from his place of business, and the story had all the earmarks of being feature material. Some six witnesses had seen a blue globe drop silently onto a cornfield, and then take off again minutes afterward.

So Bill Dover investigated, talking to everyone of the half-dozen witnesses. He talked to three children, who giggled throughout the interview, until he gave up in disgust. He talked to an itinerant named Sawdust, who breathed fumes that were sixty-percent mule, thirty-percent rye, and ten-percent hair tonic. He talked to a sullen short-order cook named Jeff, whose friends had ribbed him unmercifully, sealing his lips. Finally, weary of the whole business, Dover talked to a squint-eyed farmer named Calkins, whose cornfield had been the landing site.

"Nope," he said, scratching his chin. "Didn't actually see this here blue globe *land*. Thought I saw somethin' takin' *off*, though, but it was goin' mighty fast. Sort of a blur."

"Oh," Bill Dover said.

"Funniest thing was the man," the farmer said, after a pause. "Beats me how a man got there."

"Got where?"

"In my cornfield, right after this thing happened. Walkin' across the field. Darned if I know how he got there. Weren't there before."

Dover's pulse did a mambo. "What did he look like?"

"Oh, just a man. Two arms, two legs, like everybody else. He walked straight across the north forty and outta sight."

"What's beyond your property? Where the man went?"

"Public highway."

Dover did some chin scratching of his own. "Thanks a lot, Mr. Calkins," he said. "Thanks very much."

Back in the small hotel room where he had made his headquarters, William Dover spent an unprofitable hour in thought, trying to determine his next move. He could give it up, of course, and return to the news service with the report of another failure. But the idea of facing the ill-concealed grins and smothered chuckles of be staff members was too intolerable.

He went out for an unappetizing meal in the hotel dining room. He finished it hastily, bought a local paper, and returned to his room.

He found the item on page four.

*MENTAL CASE FOUND ON HIGHWAY;*
*MAY HAVE ESCAPED FROM SANITORIUM*
*Hillsboro, March 10, State troopers patrolling Highway 102 today discovered an unidentified man, about thirty-five years of age, wandering*

*down the center of the road. He was taken into custody as a hazard to traffic, but questioning produced no response. Examining police physician Dr. John Morrisey declared that the man was in a cataleptic state, and might be an escaped patient from the Wharton Sanatorium in Grover, Tennessee, a private institution for the mentally ill. No contact has yet been made to the Wharton home due to a telephone power failure caused by the recent storm.*

Dover got excited.

A strange, cataleptic man, wandering on a public highway.

It could be a coincidence, or it could be a story. He picked up the telephone and called the newspaper itself. He got a rather laconic reception at first, until he dropped the name of the News Service; then someone shouted to somebody else at the other end, and in a few minutes, he was in possession of the pertinent facts.

He learned that the unidentified man had been driven to the Wharton Sanatorium by the state police. The authorities there had taken the man into their confinement, but the newspaper hadn't yet learned whether he was a newcomer or an escapee from the mental home. Dover got the address and even road directions to the Sanatorium, then he hung up the phone abruptly, changed his shirt, and left the hotel.

He strayed a bit in making the twenty-mile journey from Hillsboro, but then he spotted a neat little sign on the side road that lead to Wharton. It was a bad, pitted road, and he was grateful when the car at last reached the long driveway that led to the door of the small, L-shaped building that housed both inmates and medical staff.

He slammed the car door behind him, and made straight for the door marked OFFICE. A thin man with matted hair blocked his path.

"Hail, Caesar," the thin man said.

"Hail," said Dover. "Who's the boss around here?"

"Thou, almighty Caesar," said the man, with a low bow. Dover grinned at him and tried again.

"No," he said gently. "I mean the big medical boss. Who's the doctor in charge?"

"Dr. Logan, of course," the man said stiffly. "And I, dear sir, am Marcus Aurelius."

"Pleased to meet you," said Dover. He knocked at the door. There was no answer, so he turned the knob and walked in. The office was empty.

"Where's the doctor?" he asked the inmate, who had followed him.

"I know nothing," said the thin man. "You may, perhaps, learn more from the gardeners."

Dover looked around him. "Gardeners? What gardeners?"

"Around the other side," said the man.

The columnist thanked him, and the thin man accepted it with another sweeping bow. Dover walked briskly around the short side of the building, through a white gate that led to the rear of the Sanatorium.

He spotted the gardeners immediately. There were two of them, in neat gray overalls, but even their apparent industry didn't seem to have been sufficient to save the flowerbeds from being anything more than tatty and sparse. But they were certainly willing; turning over the brown soil with flying shovels.

"Hello, there," he said. "Is Dr. Logan around?"

One of the gardeners looked up at him vaguely, but the other took no notice of his presence and kept on digging.

"Who are you?" said the gardener.

"My name's Dover, Associated News Service. I'd like to speak to Dr. Logan." He turned way uneasily from the man's brilliant gaze.

"Dr. Logan will be back shortly. Would you like to help us dig meanwhile?"

Dover blinked. "I'll finesse it," he grinned weakly. "If you don't mind."

"Digging's fun," said the other, without breaking his motion.

"Don't mind him," said the first gardener. "Perhaps you'd like to supervise the work. That requires no effort, and every job should have a supervisor. Don't you agree?"

"I suppose so," said Dover uncertainly. He came a little closer to them. The man who had addressed him had already started a good, five-foot-deep hole. "Well, if you want me to supervise," he said, "isn't that a little deep for planting?"

"Perhaps," said the man haughtily. "But I *like* to dig."

"Digging's fun," said the other.

A man in a tweed jacket came around the corner of the house. Dover was relieved to see him.

"Dr. Dover?" he said, as the man approached.

"Attention!" cried the first gardener. The other snapped to, holding his shovel like a rifle.

"Cut it out," said the doctor to them cheerfully. "This isn't the army, Mr. Lydecker." The man looked hurt, and returned to his task glumly. The other followed suit. "You wanted to see me?" said the doctor.

"Yes, please," said Dover nervously. "Could we go inside?"

"Certainly." He opened a screen door that brought them into the same office Dover had tried on the other side. "Come right in."

When they were seated inside, Dover identified himself, and told the physician part of his purpose in coming to the Wharton home.

"You mean Mr. Whitney?" the doctor said. "Oh, yes. We're taking care of Mr. Whitney."

"Whitney? You know the man then?"

"Not really," smiled the doctor, reaching across the desk for a humidor. He settled back comfortably and filled his pipe, then he looked at the columnist with jovial good humor. "He wasn't a patient here. He's a stranger, but for some reason, the inmates called him Mr. Whitney when they saw him brought in, and the medical staff has adopted the name."

"What's wrong with him?"

"He's cataleptic, to begin with. What caused the catalepsy is something we don't know. Are you related to this man, did you say?"

"No, no," said Dover. "As I said, I'm a newspaper man. I'm in Hillsboro on business. I saw the newspaper account, so I decided to follow up the story."

"Well, there's very little I can tell you," said Logan. "The police have put his description out for identification and so forth. Meanwhile, we've asked to take charge of him, since he is definitely troubled. At least we can give him peace and quiet until disposition is made."

"I see," said Dover. He looked around the office, and then asked: "Do you think I could see this man?"

The doctor looked dubious. "I don't know about that," he said. "As I told you, he's a very sick man. He shouldn't be unduly disturbed."

"I won't disturb him," the columnist promised. "I just want a look. Perhaps I can help identify him," he added, knowing full well that he could not.

"Well..." The doctor tamped his pipe. "You did make a long trip, and anyone who braves that old dirt road deserves consideration." He grinned widely. "All right," he said. "Just a look now."

As they went through the doorway once more, Dover asked about the industrious gardeners. The doctor laughed.

"Dedicated, aren't they?" he said. "They'll be digging up all the grounds if we don't put a check on their enthusiasm. However, it's good therapy, if you know anything about this sort of thing."

They came to the door that opened into the patient's quarters of the Wharton Sanatorium. As the doctor reached for the handle, a spry little man appeared and opened the door for him.

"Thank you, Mr. Spear," said the doctor.

"My pleasure, sir," said the inmate. "And I see you have with you the celebrated brain surgeon, Dr. Cushman."

"No," the doctor chuckled. "This is Mr. Dover."

"Very wise," said the little man, winking owlishly. "Incognito, eh? Very wise, Dr. Cushman."

"And how is your knitting, Mr. Spear?" said the doctor.

"Fine, fine," said the little man. "Mr. Braniff is terribly jealous, of course. Thinks he can do it better. Ta-ta," he said suddenly, and broke into a quick-legged run.

Logan looked after him and snorted humorously. "Interesting man, Mr. Spear," he said. "But I suppose you're more interested in our Mr. Whitney."

"Yes," said Dover.

"He's right in here."

The man was in a small, barely furnished room, with barred windows. He was lying on a narrow cot, hands clenched at his sides, wide eyes staring sightlessly at the ceiling. Dover was disappointed. He was definitely no monster. He had two arms and two legs, just like everybody else.

"Pitiful, isn't it?" said Logan softly. "Do you recognize him, Mr. Dover?"

"No," said the columnist. "I never saw him before."

"Poor fellow must have a terrible shock," said the doctor. "We have to feed him, dress him—just like a child."

"Awful," said Dover.

When they closed the door quietly behind them, the columnist decided to confide in the physician.

"I guess I've gone as far as I can on this thing," he sighed. "So I'd like to tell you just why I was interested in this man, Dr. Logan. You may think I'm cra—you may think I'm pretty silly when you hear my reason for coming here."

"Do tell me," the doctor urged. "I'd be very interested."

"Well," said Dover tentatively. "I don't know if you've heard about that—well, that object that was supposed to have landed in Hillsboro a week or so ago."

"Seem to recall something. Another Saucer story, wasn't it?"

"Yes. One of those. Only I got the idea somehow—don't ask me why—that there might be something to this story. After all, it's not impossible for a spaceship to land—"

"No, not impossible," the doctor agreed warmly.

"Well, one of the accounts I heard—I'd rather not say where—indicated that there might have been a *man* who walked away from the globe after its descent."

"I see," said Logan.

"So when I saw the news item—about the wandering mental case, you understand—I put two and two together."

"And the result?" said the doctor.

"Zero, I guess," said the columnist sourly. "At any rate, so it appears. Unless, of course, there's another explanation—"

"What do you mean?"

They were back at the physician's office, and Dover waited until they were reseated inside before he broke his newly formed theory.

"Look," he said eagerly. "Suppose—just suppose now, for the sake of argument—that a spaceship *did* land in the Hillsboro cornfield."

"Okay," said the doctor grinning. "Let's suppose that."

"All right," said Dover. "Now let's also suppose that a man from another planet got *off* that ship."

"Whoops," laughed the doctor. "Now you've lost me."

"It's not incredible," Dover insisted. "Evolution says this is the shape for intelligence," he continued, indicating his own body. "And space travel calls for high intelligence, doesn't it? So why couldn't this outer-space creature look exactly like us?"

"Okay," said the doctor. "I'll buy it for the time being."

"Now," said Dover intensely, "what happens when our space passenger gets off the bus? Is he pleased and happy at finding this new world? Is he fit as a fiddle? Or is he maybe so badly shaken up by the whole thing that he lands in a state of shock?"

"Really, now," said Logan.

"No, hear me out," said Dover. "Maybe he's in a state resembling catalepsy, just like Mr. Whitney. After all, it's quite an experience, isn't it? And maybe the landing he made was all wrong—maybe he made a blunder—"

"Well," said the doctor, "it's *one* idea…"

"Now what would happen to such a man?" said Dover enthusiastically. "Would he be *recognized* for what he was? Or would the authorities merely assume—and justly, Dr. Logan, don't misunderstand—merely assume that he was a mental case, and bustle him off to a Sanatorium?"

"Like Wharton, for instance?"

"Like Wharton," said Dover.

"Really—" the doctor began.

"Don't jump on me," the columnist pleaded. "I'm not saying your Mr. Whitney is an interplanetary visitor. God knows I don't have any evidence. But can't you see the possibilities?"

The doctor stood up.

"You," he said, "have quite an imagination. I, on the other hand, am something of a dull fellow, Mr. Dover."

"Don't get me wrong," Dover said anxiously. "I'm sure you know your business, Dr. Logan. But just look at it with an open mind—"

"I'm all for that, of course. But yours is the kind of dreaming that's best done in the Sunday papers, Mr. Dover. Not in a medical institution, where we're trying to make sick people better."

"But if you could only hear the witnesses," said Dover. "I mean, about this 'blue globe' business. It's not like all those other wild stories, Dr. Logan. There's the smell of truth around this one—"

The doctor had stopped smiling. "And just what would you want me to do about it, Mr. Dover?"

"I don't know," said the columnist bewilderedly. "Keep an eye on Whitney, I guess. See if he isn't something *more* than a mental case."

"Mr. Whitney will get all the attention he requires—"

"I don't mean that. I mean that perhaps *other* people— scientific people—might look into the case. Just on the wild chance—"

"I told you," the doctor said sharply. "At the moment, peace and quiet are essential to this man's health. I won't endanger him because of some fantastic idea—"

"But what if it's true?" said Dover desperately.

The doctor looked thoughtful. He paced the floor in front of his desk, and then turned to the columnist again.

"I'll tell you what," he said. He reached over and pressed the button on the intercom atop his desk. "Mr. Dearborn," he said, "please send in Mr. A. At once."

"Mr. A?" said Dover.

"Yes," Logan replied. "He knows a little more about Mr. Whitney than I do. Maybe he can help you further."

"Fine," said Dover.

They waited in silence for a few minutes. Then someone appeared at the office door.

"Why, it's Marcus Aurelius," he said in surprise.

"You wanted to see me, Dr. Logan?"

"Mr. A.," said the doctor, "we have a little problem. Perhaps you can help us.

"Mr. Dover here is with the newspapers, and he is very interested in our Mr. Whitney. You remember Mr. Whitney, of course."

"Yes, indeed!"

"Well, Mr. Dover has the idea that perhaps Mr. Whitney came to us from outer space. You see, there was a flying saucer landing in Hillsboro a week or two ago. Mr. Dover believes that Mr. Whitney was a passenger.

"Mr. Dover is under the impression that the authorities should be informed of this possibility. Do you understand?

"This would cause quite a disturbance, of course," said Logan. "All sorts of investigations. No peace and quiet.

"It would be a most unfortunate thing to happen at Wharton," the doctor said suavely. "Don't you agree, Mr. A.?" He waited, smiling.

"Definitely, doctor," said the thin man. His hand went into his clothing, and produced a pocketknife.

*"Dr. Logan!"* Dover shrieked, backing away.

"Such an investigation would be most unwelcome," said Logan coolly. "And it hardly seems necessary, does it?"

"Not at all," said Mr. A., advancing upon Dover.

"You see, Mr. Dover," said the physician, smiling sadly. "Not all of our landings are so clumsy. Not all of them result in Mr. Whitneys. Most of our globes descend very, very smoothly. Don't they, Mr. A.?"

"Very smoothly," said Mr. A., backing Dover up against the wall.

"Beware the Ides of March," smiled Dr. Logan.

"Beware," said Mr. A., lifting the knife.

Outside the window, the gardeners stopped digging and waited. Shortly, the doctor appeared at the window and nodded to them pleasantly.

"All right," he said.

They returned to their work, shoveling deeper, deeper.

"Digging's fun," one of the gardeners said.

## THE END

# The Meteor Girl

## By JACK WILLIAMSON

*Through the complicated space-time of the fourth dimension goes Charlie King in an attempt to rescue the Meteor Girl.*

"What's the good in Einstein, anyhow?"

I shot the question at lean young Charlie King. In a moment he looked up at me; I thought there was pain in the back of his clear brown eyes. Lips closed in a thin white line across his wind-tanned face; nervously he tapped his pipe on the metal cowling of the *Golden Gull's* cockpit.

"I know that space is curved, that there is really no space or time, but only space-time, that electricity and gravitation and magnetism are all the same. But how is that going to pay my grocery bill—or yours?"

"That's what Virginia wants to know."

"Virginia Randall?" I was astonished. "Why, I thought—"

"I know. We've been engaged a year. But she's called it off."

Charlie looked into my eyes for a long minute, his lips still compressed. We were leaning on the freshly painted, streamline fuselage of the *Golden Gull*, as neat a little amphibian monoplane as ever made three hundred miles an hour. She stood on the glistening white sand of our private landing field on the eastern Florida coast. Below us the green Atlantic was running in white foam on the rocks.

In the year that Charlie King and I had been out of the Institute of Technology, we had built the nucleus of a commercial airplane business. We had designed and built here in our own shops several very successful seaplanes and amphibians. Charlie's brilliant mathematical mind was of the greatest aid, except when he was too far lost in his abstruse speculations to descend to things commercial. Mathematics is painful enough to me when it is used in calculating the camber of an airplane wing. And pure mathematics, such as the theories of relativity and equivalence, I simply abhor.

I was amazed. Virginia Randall was a girl trim and beautiful as our shining *Golden Gull*. I had thought them devotedly in love, and had been looking forward to the wedding.

"But it isn't two weeks, since Virginia was out here. You took her up in our *Western Gull IV*."

Nervously Charlie lit his pipe, drew quickly on it. His face, lean and drawn beneath the flying goggles pushed up on his forehead, sought mine anxiously.

"I know. I drove her back to the station. That was when—when we quarreled."

"But why? About Einstein? That's silly."

"She wanted me to give it up here, and go in with her father in his Wall Street brokerage business. The old gent is willing to take me, and make a business man of me."

"Why, I couldn't run the business without you, Charlie!"

"We talked about that, Hammond. I don't really do much of the work. Just play around with the mathematics, and leave the models and blueprints to you."

"Oh, Charlie, that's not quite—"

"It's the truth, right enough," he said, bitterly. "You design aircraft, and I play with Einstein. And as you say, a fellow can't eat equations."

"I'd hate to see you go."

"And I'd hate to give up you, and our business, and the math. Really no need of it. My tastes are simple enough. And old 'Iron-clad' Randall has made all one family needs. Virginia's not exactly a pauper, herself. Two or three millions, I think."

"And where did Virginia go?"

"She took the *Valhalla* yesterday at San Francisco. Going to join her father at Panama. He cruises about the world in his steam yacht, you know, and runs Wall Street by radio. I was to telegraph her if I'd changed my mind. I decided to stick to you, Hammond. I telegraphed a corsage of orchids, and sent her the message, 'Einstein forever!'"

"If I know Virginia, those were not very politic words."

"Well, a man—"

His words were cut short by a very unusual incident.

A thin, high scream came suddenly from above our neat stuccoed hangars at the edge of the white field. I looked up quickly, to catch a glimpse of a bright object hurtling through the air above our heads. The bellowing scream ended abruptly in a thunderous crash. I felt a tremor of the ground underfoot.

"What—" I ejaculated.

*"Look,"* cried Charlie.

He pointed. I looked over the gleaming metal wing of the *Golden Gull*, to see a huge cloud of white sand rising like a fountain at the farther side of the level field. Deliberately the column of debris rose, spread, rained down, leaving a gaping crater in the earth.

"Something fell?"

"It sounded like a shell from a big gun, except that it didn't explode. Let's get over and see."

We ran to where the thing had struck, three hundred yards across the field. We found a great funnel-shaped pit torn in the naked earth. It was a dozen yards across, fifteen feet deep, and surrounded with a powdery ring of white sand and pulverized rock.

"Something like a shell-hole," I observed.

"I've got it!" Charlie cried. "It was a meteor!"

"A meteor? So big?"

"Yes. Lucky for us it was no bigger. If it had been like the one that fell in Siberia a few years ago, or the one that made the Winslow crater in Arizona—we wouldn't have been talking about it. Probably we have a chunk of nickel-iron alloy here."

"I'll get some of the men out here with digging tools, and we'll see what we can find."

Our mechanics were already hurrying across the field. I shouted at them to bring picks and shovels. In a few minutes five of us were at work throwing sand and shattered rock out of the pit.

Suddenly I noticed a curious thing. A pale bluish mist hung in the bottom of the pit. It was easily transparent, no denser than tobacco smoke. Passing my spade through it did not seem to disturb it in the least.

I rubbed my eyes doubtfully, said to Charlie, "Do you see a sort of blue haze in the pit?"

He peered. "No. No... Yes. Yes, I do! Funny thing. Kind of a blue fog. And the tools cut right through it without moving it! Queer! Must have something to do with the meteor!" He was very excited.

We dug more eagerly. An hour later we had opened the hole to a depth of twenty feet. Our shovels were clanging on the gray iron of the rock from space. The mist had grown thicker as the excavation deepened; we looked at the stone through a screen of motionless blue fog.

We had found the meteor. There were several queer things about it. The first man who touched it—a big Swede mechanic named Olson—was knocked cold as if by a nasty jolt of electricity. It took half an hour to bring him to consciousness.

As fast as the rugged iron side of the meteorite was uncovered, a white crust of frost formed over it.

"It was as cold as outer space, nearly at the absolute zero," Charlie explained. "And it was heated only superficially during its quick passage through the air. But how it comes to be charged with electricity—I can't say."

He hurried up to his laboratory behind the hangars, where he had equipment ranging from an astronomical telescope to a delicate seismograph. He brought back as much electrical equipment as he could carry. He had me touch an insulated wire to the frost-covered stone from space, while he put the other end to one post of a galvanometer.

I think he got a current that wrecked the instrument. At any rate, he grew very much excited.

"Something queer about that stone," he cried. "This is the chance of a lifetime. I don't know that a meteor has ever been scientifically examined so soon after falling."

He hurried us all across to the laboratory. We came back with a truck load of coils and tubes and batteries and potentiometers and other assorted equipment. He had men with heavy robber gloves lift the frost-covered stone to a packing box on a bench. The thing was irregular in shape, about a foot long; it must have weighed two hundred pounds. He sent a man racing on a motorcycle to the drug store to get dry ice (solidified carbon dioxide) to keep the iron stone at its low temperature.

In a few hours he had a complete laboratory set up around the meteorite. He worked feverishly in the hot sunshine, reading the various instruments he had set up, and arranging more. He contrived to keep the stone cold by packing it in a box of dry ice.

The mechanics stopped for dinner, and I tried to get him to take time to eat.

"No, Hammond," he said. "This is something big! We were talking about Einstein. This rock seems energized with a new kind of force: all meteors are probably the same way, when they first plunge out of space. I think this will be to relativity what the falling apple is to gravity. This is a big thing."

He looked up at me, brown eyes flashing.

"This is my chance to make a name, Hammond. If I do something big enough—Virginia might reconsider her opinion."

Charlie worked steadily through the long hot afternoon. I spent most of the time helping him, or gazing in fascination at the curious haze of luminous blue mist that clung like a sphere of azure fog about the meteoric stone. I did not completely understand what he did; the reader who wants the details may consult the monograph he is preparing for the scientific press.

He had the men string up a line from our direct current generator in the shops, to supply power for his electrical instruments. He mounted a powerful electromagnet just below the meteorite, and set up an X-ray tube to bombard it with rays.

Night came, and the fire of the white sun faded from the sky. In the darkness, the curious haze about the stone became luminescent, distinct, a dim, motionless sphere of blue light. I fancied that I saw grotesque shapes flashing through it. A ball of blue fire, shimmering and ghost-like, shrouded the instruments.

Charlie's induction coil buzzed wickedly, with purple fire playing about the terminals. The X-ray tube flickered with a greenish glow. He manipulated the rheostat that controlled the current through the electromagnet, and continued to read his instruments.

"Look at *that*," he cried.

The bluish haze about the stone grew brighter; it became a ball of sapphire flame, five feet thick, bright and motionless.

A great sphere of shimmering azure fire. Wisps of pale, sparkling bluish mist ringed it. The stone in its box, the X-ray bulb and other apparatus were hidden. The end of the table stuck oddly from the ball of light.

I heard Charlie move a switch. The hum of the coils changed a note.

The ball of blue fire vanished abruptly. It became a hole, a window in space.

Through it, we saw another world…

The darkness of the night hung about us. Where the ball had been was a circle of misty blue flame, five feet across. Through that circle I could see a vast expanse of blue ocean, running in high, white-capped rollers, beneath a sky overcast with low gray clouds.

It was no flat picture like a movie screen. The scene had vast depth; I knew that we were really looking over an infinite expanse of stormy ocean. It was all perfectly clear, distinct…real.

Astounded, I turned to find Charlie standing back and looking into the ring of blue fire, with a curious mixture of surprise and delighted satisfaction.

"What—what—" I gasped.

"It's amazing! Wonderful! More than I had dared hope for! The complete vindication of my theory! If Virginia cares for scientific reputation—"

"But what is it?"

"It's hard to explain without mathematical language. You might say that we are looking through a hole in space. The new force in the meteorite, amplified by the X-rays and the magnetic field, is causing a distortion of space-time coordinates. You know that a gravitational field bends light; the light of a star is deflected in passing the sun. The field of this meteorite bends light through space-time, through the four-dimensional continuum. That scrap of ocean we can see may be on the other side of the earth."

I walked around the circle of luminous smoke with the marvelous picture in the center. It seemed that the window swung with me. I surveyed the whole angry surface of that slate-gray, storm-beaten sea, to the misty horizon. Nowhere was it broken by land or ship.

Charlie fell to adjusting his rheostat and switches.

It seemed that the gray ocean moved swiftly beyond the window. Vast stretches of it raced below our eyes. Faint black stains of steamer smoke appeared against the blue-gray horizon and swept past. Then land appeared—a long, green-gray line. We had a flash of a long coast that unreeled in endless panorama before us. It was such a view as one might get from a swift airplane—a plane flying thousands of miles per hour.

The Golden Gate flashed before us, with the familiar skyline of San Francisco rising on the hills behind it.

"San Francisco," Charlie cried. "This is the Pacific we've been seeing. Let's find the *Valhalla*. We might be able to see Virginia…"

The coast-line vanished as he manipulated his instruments. Staring into the circle of shining blue mist, I saw the endless ocean racing below us again. We picked up a pleasure yacht, running under bare poles.

"I didn't know there was such a storm on," Charlie murmured.

Other vessels swam past below us, laboring against heavy seas.

Then we looked upon an ocean whipped into mighty white-crowned waves. Rain beat down in sheets from low dense clouds; vivid violet lightnings flashed before us. It seemed very strange to see such lightning and hear not the faintest whisper of thunder—but no sound came from anything we saw through the blue-rimmed window in space.

"I hope the *Valhalla* isn't in weather like *this*," cried Charlie.

In a few minutes a dark form loomed through the wind driven mist. Swiftly it swam nearer; became a black ship.

"Only a tramp," Charlie said, breathing a sigh of relief.

It was a dingy tramp steamer, her superstructure wrecked. Her fires seemed dead. She lay across the wind, rolling sluggishly, threatening to sink with every monstrous wave. We saw no living person aboard her; she seemed a sinking derelict. We made out the name *Roma* on her side.

Charlie moved his dials again.

In a few minutes the slender prow of another great steamer came through the sheets of rain. It was evidently a passenger vessel. She seemed limping along, half-wrecked, with mighty waves breaking over her rail.

Charlie grew white with alarm. "The *Valhalla*," he gasped. "And she's headed straight for that wreck!"

In a moment, as he brought the liner closer below our blue-rimmed window, I, too, made out the name. The wet, glistening decks were almost deserted. Here and there a man struggled futilely against the force of the storm.

In a few minutes the drifting wreck of the *Roma* came into our view, dead ahead of the limping liner. Through the mist and falling rain, the derelict could not have been in sight of the lookout of the passenger vessel until she was almost upon it.

We saw the white burst of steam as the siren was blown. We watched the desperate effort of the liner to check her way, to come about. But it was too much for the already crippled ship. Charlie cried out as a mighty wave drove the *Valhalla* down upon the sluggishly drifting wreck.

All the mad scene that ensued was strangely silent. We heard no crash when the collision occurred; heard no screams or shouts while the mob of desperate, white-faced passengers were fighting their way to the deck. The vain struggle to launch the boats was like a silent movie.

One boat was splintered while being lowered. Another, already filled with passengers, was lifted by a great wave and crushed against the side of the ship. Only shivered wood and red foam were left. The ship listed so rapidly that the boats on the lee side were useless. It was impossible to launch the others in that terrible, lashing sea.

"Virginia can swim," Charlie said hopefully. "You know she tried the Channel last year, and nearly made it, too."

He stopped to watch that terrible scene in white-faced, anxious silence.

The tramp went down before the steamer, drawing fragments of wrecked boats after it. The liner was evidently sinking rapidly. We saw dozens of hopeless, panic-stricken passengers diving off the lee side, trying to swim off far enough to avoid the tremendous suction.

Then, with a curious deliberation, the bow of the *Valhalla* dipped under green water; her stern rose in the air until the ship stood almost perpendicular. She slipped quickly down, out of sight.

Only a few swimming humans, and the wrecks of a few boats, were left on the rough gray sea. Charlie fumbled nervously with his dials, trying to get the scene near enough so that we could see the identity of the struggling swimmers.

A long boat, which must have been swept below by the suction of the ship, came plunging above the surface, upside down. It drifted swiftly among the swimmers, who struggled to reach it. I saw one person, evidently a girl, grasp it and drag herself upon it. It swept on past the few others still struggling.

The wrecked boat with the girl upon it seemed to be coming swiftly toward our blue-rimmed window. In a few minutes I saw something familiar about her.

"It's Virginia!" Charlie cried. "God! We've got to save her, somehow..."

The long rollers drove the over-turned boat swiftly along. Virginia Randall clung desperately to it, deluged in foam, whipped with flying spray, the wild wind tearing at her.

About us, the clear still night was deepening. The air was warm and still; the hot stars shone steadily. Quiet lighted houses were in sight above the beach. It was very strange to look through the fire-rimmed circle, to see a girl struggling for life, clinging to a wrecked boat in a stormy sea.

Charlie watched in an apathy of grief and horror, trembling and speechless doing nothing except move the controls to keep the floating girl in our sight.

Hours went by as we watched. Then Charlie cried out in sudden hope. "There's a chance! I might do it! I might be able to save her!"

"Might do what?"

"We are able to see what we do because the field of the meteor bends light through the four-dimensional continuum. The world line of a ray of light is a geodesic in the continuum. The field I have built distorts the continuum, so we see rays that originated at a distant point. Is that clear?"

"Clear as mud."

"Well, anyhow, if the field were strong enough, we could bring physical objects through space-time, instead of mere visual images. We could pick Virginia up and bring her right here to the crater. I'm sure of it."

"You mean you could move a girl through some four or five thousand miles of space?"

"You don't understand. She wouldn't come through space at all, but through space-time, through the continuum, which is a very different thing. She is four thousand miles away in our three-dimensional space, but in space-time, as you see, she is only a few yards away. She is only a few yards from us in the fourth dimension. If I can increase the field a little, she will be drawn right through."

"You're a wizard if you can do it..."

"I've got to do it. She's a fine swimmer—that's the only reason she's still alive—but she'll never live to reach the shore. Not in a sea like that."

Charlie fell to work at once, mounting another electromagnet beside the one he had set up, and rigging up two more X-ray bulbs beside the packing box, which held the meteor. The motion of the boat in the fire-rimmed window kept drawing it swiftly away from us, and Charlie showed me how to move the dial of his rheostat to keep the girl in view.

Before he had completed his arrangements, a patch of white foam came into view just ahead of the drifting boat. In a moment I made out a cruel black rock, with the angry sea breaking into fleecy spray upon it. The boat was almost upon it, driving straight for it. Charlie saw it, and cried out in horror.

The long black hull of the splintered boat, floating keel upward, was only a few yards away. A great white-capped breaker lifted it and hurled it forward, with the girl clinging to it. She drew herself up and stared in terror at the black rock, while another long surging roller picked up the boat and swept it forward again.

I stood, paralyzed in horror, while the shattered boat was driven full upon the great rock. I could imagine the crash of it, but it was all as still as a silent picture. The boat, riding high on a crest of white foam, smashed against the rock and was shivered to splinters. Virginia was hurled forward against the slick wet stone. Desperately she scrambled to reach the top of the boulder. Her hands slipped on the polished rock;

the wild sea dragged at her. At last she got out of reach of the angry gray water, though spume still deluged her.

I breathed a sigh of relief, though her position was still far from enviable.

"Virginia! Virginia! Why did I let you go?" Charlie cried.

Desperately he fell to work again, mounting the magnet and tubes. Another hour went by, while I watched the shivering girl on the rock. Bobbed hair, wet and glistening, was plastered close against her head, and her clothing was torn half off. She looked utterly exhausted; it seemed to take all her ebbing energy to cling to the rock against the force of the wind and the waves that dashed against her. She looked cold, blue and trembling.

The water stood higher.

"The tide is rising," Charlie exclaimed. "It will cover the rock pretty soon. If I don't get her off in time—she's lost."

He finished twisting his wires together.

"I've got it all ready," he said. "Now, I've got to find out exactly where she is, to know how to set it. Even then it's fearfully uncertain. I hate to try it, but it's the only chance.

"You can find out?"

"Yes. From the spectral shift and other factors. I'll have to get some other apparatus." He ran up to the laboratory, across the level field that lay black beneath the stars. He came back, panting, with spectrometer, terrestrial globe, and other articles.

"The tide is higher," he cried as he looked through the blue-rimmed circle at the girl on the rock. "She'll be swept off before long!"

He mounted the spectrometer and fell to work with a will, taking observations through the telescope, adjusting prisms and diffraction gratings, reading electrometers and other apparatus, and stopping to make intricate calculations.

I helped him when I could, or stared through the ring of shining blue mist, where I could see the waves breaking higher about the exhausted girl who clung to the rock. Clouds of wind-whipped spray often hid her from sight. I knew that she would not have the strength to hold on much longer against the force of the rising sea.

Although driven almost to distraction by the horror of her predicament, he worked with a cool, swift efficiency. Only the pale, anxiety-drawn expression on his face showed how great was the strain. He finished the last spectrometer observation, snatched out a pad and fell to figuring furiously.

"Something queer here," he said presently, frowning. "A shift of the spectrum that I can't explain by distortion through three-dimensional space alone. I don't understand it."

We stared at the chilled and trembling girl on the rock.

"I'm almost afraid to try it. What if something went wrong?"

He turned to the terrestrial globe he had brought down and traced a line over it. He made a quick calculation on his pad, then made a fine dot on the globe with the pencil point.

"Here she is. On a rock some miles off Point Eugenia, on the coast of the Mexican State of Lower California. Most lonely spot in the world. No chance for a rescue. We must—

"My god!" he screamed in sudden horror. "Look!"

I looked through the blue-ringed window and saw the girl. Green water was surging about her waist. It seemed that each wave almost tore her off. Then I saw that she was struggling with something. A great coiling tentacle, black and leathery and glistening, was thrust up out of the green water. It wavered deliberately through the air and grasped at the girl. She seemed to scream, though we could hear nothing. She beat at the monster, weakly, vainly.

"She's gone," cried Charlie.

"An octopus," I said. "A giant cuttlefish…"

Virginia made a sudden fierce effort. With a strength that I had not thought her chilled limbs possessed, she tore away from the dreadful creature and clambered higher on the rock. But still a hideous black tentacle clung about her ankle, tugging at her, drawing her back despite her desperate struggle to break free.

"I've got to try it," Charlie said, determination flashing in his eyes. "It's a chance…"

He closed a switch. His new coils sung out above the old one. X-ray tubes flickered beside the blue fire that ringed the window. He adjusted his rheostats and closed the circuit through the new magnet.

A curtain of blue flame was drawn quickly between us and the round, fire-rimmed window. A huge ball of blue fire hung about the meteorite and the instruments. For minutes it hung there, while Charlie, perspiring, worked desperately with the apparatus. Then it expanded; became huge. It exploded noiselessly, in a great flash of sapphire flame, then vanished completely.

Meteor, bench, and apparatus were gone.

In the light of the stars we could make out the huge crater the meteorite had torn, with a few odds and ends of equipment scattered about it. But all the apparatus Charlie had set up, connected with the meteoric stone, had disappeared.

He was dumbfounded, staggered with disappointment.

"Virginia! Virginia!" he called out, in a hopeless tone. "No, she isn't here. It didn't draw her through. I've failed. And we can't even see her any more…"

Desperately I searched for consolation for him.

"Maybe the octopus won't hurt her," I offered. "They say that most of the stories of their ferocity are somewhat exaggerated."

"If the monster doesn't get her, the tide will," he said bitterly. "I made a miserable failure of it. And I don't know why! I can't understand it."

Apathetically, he picked up his pad and held it in the light of his electric lantern.

"Something funny about this equation. The shift of the spectrum lines can't be accounted for by distortion through space alone."

With wrinkled brow, he stared for many minutes at the bit of paper he held in the white circle of light. Suddenly he seized a pencil and figured rapidly.

"I have it! The light was bent through time! I should have recognized these space-time coordinates."

He calculated again.

"Yes. The scene we saw in that circle of light was distant from us not only in space but in time. The *Valhalla* probably hasn't sunk yet at all. We were looking into the future!"

"But how can that be? Seeing things before they happen?"

I have the profoundest respect for Charlie King's mathematical genius. But when he said that I was frankly incredulous.

"Space and time are only relative terms. Our material universe is merely the intersection of tangled world lines of geodesics in a four-dimensional continuum. Space and time have no meaning independently of each other. Jeans says. 'A terrestrial astronomer may reckon that the outburst on Nova Persei occurred a century before the great fire of London, but an astronomer on the Nova may reckon with equal accuracy that the great fire occurred a century before the outburst on the Nova.' The field of this meteorite deflected light waves so that we saw them earlier, according to our conventional ideas of time, than they originated. We saw several hours into the future.

"And the amplified field of the magnet, though strong enough to move Virginia through space, was not sufficiently powerful to draw her back to us across time. Yet she must have felt the pull. Some dreadful thing may have happened. The problem is rather complicated."

He lifted his pencil again. In the glow of the little electric lantern I saw his lean young face tense with the fierce effort of his thought. His pencil raced across the little pad, setting down symbols that I could make nothing of.

My own thoughts were racing. Seeing into the future was a rather revolutionary idea to me. My mind is conservative; I have always been skeptical of the more fantastic ideas suggested by science. But Charlie seemed to know what he was talking about. In view of the marvelous things he had done that night, it seemed hardly fair to doubt him now. I decided to accept his astounding statement at face value and to follow the adventure through.

He lifted his pencil and consulted the luminous dial of his wristwatch.

"We saw that last scene some twelve hours and forty minutes before it happened—to put it in conventional language. The distortion of the time coordinates amounted to that."

In the light of dawn—for we had been all night at the meteor pit, and silver was coming in the east—he looked at me with fierce resolve in his eyes.

"Hammond, that gives us over twelve hours to get to Virginia."

"You mean to go? But just twelve hours? That's better than the transcontinental record—to say nothing of the time it would take to find a little rock in the Pacific."

"We have the *Golden Gull.* She's as fast as any ship we've ever flown."

"But we can't take the *Gull.* Those alterations haven't been made. And that new engine... A bear-cat for power, but it may go dead any second. The *Gull* can fly, but she isn't safe."

"Safety be damned! I've got to get to Virginia, and get there in the next twelve hours!"

"The *Gull* will fly, but—"

"All right. Please help me get off."

"Help you off? It's a fool thing to do! But if you go, I go."

"Thanks, Hammond. Awfully!" He gripped my hand. "We've got to make it!"

With a last glance into the gaping pit from which we had dug the marvelous stone, we turned and ran across to the hangars. As we ran the sun came above the sea in the east, its first rays struck us like a fiery lance. The mechanics had not yet appeared. Charlie pushed the doors back, and we ran out the trim little *Golden Gull,* beautiful with her slender wing and her graceful, tapering lines.

I seized the starting crank and Charlie sprang into the cockpit. I cranked until the mechanism was droning dismally, and pulled the lever that engaged it with the engine. I had been in too much haste to get up the proper speed, and the powerful new engine failed to fire. Charlie almost cried with vexation while I was cranking again.

This time the motor coughed and fell into a steady, vibrant roar. With the wind from the propeller screaming about me, I disengaged the crank and stood waiting while the motor warmed. Charlie gave it scant time to do so before he motioned me to kick out the blocks. I tumbled into the enclosed cockpit beside him, he gave the ship the gun, and we roared across the field.

In five minutes we were flying west, at a speed just under three hundred miles per hour. Charlie was crouched over the stick, scanning the instrument board, and flying the *Gull* almost at her top speed. Again and again his eyes went to the little clock on the panel.

"Twelve hours and forty minutes," he said. "And an hour gone already. We've got to be there by five minutes after six."

We were flying over Louisiana when the oil line clogged. The engine heated dangerously. Reluctantly, Charlie cut off the ignition, and fell in a swift spiral to an open field.

"We're got to fix it," he said. "Another hour gone. And we needed every minute..."

"This new engine. It's powerful enough, but we should have had time to overhaul it, and make those changes."

Charlie landed with his usual skill, and we fell to work in desperate haste. A grizzled farmer, a wad of tobacco in his cheek and three ragged urchins at his heels, stopped to watch us. He had just been to his mailbox, and had a morning paper in his hand. Charlie questioned him about the storm.

"Storm-center nears the American coast," he read in a nasal drawl. "Greatest storm of year drives shipping upon west coast. Six vessels reported lost. *S. S. Valhalla*, disabled, sends S. O. S.

"A thousand lives are the estimated toll tonight of the most terrific storm of the year, which is sweeping toward the Pacific coast, driving all shipping before it. Radiograms from the *Valhalla* at 5 p.m. report that she is disabled and in danger. It is doubtful that rescue vessels can reach her through the storm."

We got the engine repaired, took off again. Charlie looked at the little clock.

"Five minutes to ten. Eight hours and ten minutes left, and we've got a darn long ways to go."

We had to stop at San Antonio, Texas, to replenish gasoline and oil.

"Ten minutes lost." Charlie complained as we took off. "And that monster—waiting in the future to drag Virginia to a hideous death…"

Two hours later the plane developed trouble in the ignition system. The motor was new, with several radical changes that we had introduced to increase power and lessen weight. As I had objected to Charlie, we had not done enough experimental work on it to perfect it.

We limped into the field at El Paso and spent another priceless half-hour at work. I got some sandwiches at a luncheon counter beside the field, and listened a moment to a radio loudspeaker there.

"Many thousands are dead," came the crisp, metallic voice of the announcer, "as a result of the storm now raging on the Pacific coast, the worst in several years. The storm-center is spending its force on the coastal regions today. Millions of dollars in damage are reported in cities from San Francisco to Manzanillo, Mexico.

"The greatest disaster of the storm is the loss of the passenger liner *Valhalla*, of the Red Star Line. It is believed to have collided with the abandoned hulk of an Italian-owned tramp freighter, the *Roma*, which was left by its crew yesterday in a sinking condition. Radiograms from the liner ceased three hours ago, when she was said to be sinking. The officers doubted that her boats could be launched in such a sea—"

I waited to hear no more. Charlie checked our route while we were stopped. And we took off; we crossed the Rio Grande and flew across the rocky, brush-scattered hills of Mexico, in a direct line for the rock in the sea.

"If anything happens so we have to land again—well, it's just too bad," Charlie said grimly. "But we've got to go this way. It's something over six hundred miles in a straight line. Fifteen minutes to four, now. We have to average nearly three hundred miles an hour to get there."

He was silent and intent over his maps and instruments as we flew on over the lofty Sierra Madre Range, and over a long slope down to the Gulf of California. Head-winds beset us as we were over the stretch of blue water, and we flew on into a storm.

"We had hardly time to make it, without the wind against us," Charlie said. "If it holds us back many miles—well, it just mustn't."

Purple lightning flickered ominously in the mass of blue storm-clouds that hung above the mountainous peninsula of Lower California. I had a qualm about flying into it in our untested machine. But Charlie leaned tensely forward and sent the *Golden Gull* on at the limit of her speed. Gray vapor swirled about us, rent with livid streaks of lightning. Thunder crashed and rumbled above the roar of our racing engine. Wild winds screeched in the struts; rain and hail beat against us. The plane rose and fell; she was swirled about like a falling leaf. The stick struggled in Charlie's hands like a living thing. With lips tightened to a thin line, he fought silently, fiercely, desperately.

Suddenly we were sucked down until I had an uneasy feeling at the pit of my stomach. I saw the grim outline of a bare mountain peak dangerously close below us, shrouded in wind-whipped mist.

In sudden alarm I shouted, "We'd better get out of this, Charlie! We can't live in it long!"

In the roar of the storm he did not hear me, and I shouted again.

He turned to face me, after a glance at the clock. "We've less than an hour, Hammond. We've got to go on!"

I sank back in my seat. The plane rolled and tossed until I thanked my lucky stars for the safety strap. In nervous anxiety I watched Charlie bring the ship up again, and fight his way on through the storm. For an eternity, it seemed, we battled through a chaos of wind-driven mist, bright with purple lightning and shaken with crashing thunder.

Charlie struggled with the controls until he was dripping with perspiration. He must have been utterly worn out, after thirty-six hours of exhausting effort. A dozen times I despaired of life. The compass had gone to spinning crazily; we dived through the rain until we could pick up landmarks below. Three times a great bare peak loomed suddenly up ahead of us, and Charlie averted collision only by zooming suddenly upward.

Then slate-gray water was beneath us, running in white-crested waves. I knew that we were at last over the Pacific.

"We've passed Point Eugenia," Charlie said. "It can't be far, now. But we have only fifteen minutes left. Fifteen minutes to get to her—before the attraction of the meteor jerks her away, perhaps to a horrible fate."

We flew low and fast over the racing waves. Charlie looked over his charts and made a swift calculation. He changed our course a bit and we flew on at top speed. We scanned the vast, mad expanse of sea below the blue-gray clouds. Here and there were lines of white breakers, but nowhere did we see a rock with a girl upon it. Presently the green outline of an island appeared out of the wild water on our right.

"That's Del Tiburon," Charlie said. "We missed the rock."

He swung the plane about and we flew south over the hastening waves. I looked at the little clock. It showed two minutes to six. I turned to Charlie.

"Seven minutes," he whispered grimly.

On and on we flew, in a wide circle. The motor roared loud. An endless expanse of racing waves unreeled below us. The little hand crawled around the dial. One minute past six. Only four minutes to go.

We saw a speck of white foam on the mad gray water. It was miles away, almost on the horizon. We plunged toward it, motor bellowing loud. Five miles a minute we flew. The white fleck became a black rock smothered in snowy foam. On we swept, and over the rock, with bullet-like speed.

As we plunged by, I saw Virginia's slender form, tattered, brine-soaked, straggling in the hideous tentacles of the monster octopus. It was the same terrible scene that we had viewed, through the amazing phenomenon of distortion of light through space-time, four thousand miles away and twelve hours before.

In a few minutes the time would come when Charlie had ended our view of the scene by his attempt to draw the girl through the fourth dimension to our apparatus in Florida. What terrible thing might happen then?

Charlie brought the ship about so quickly that we were flung against the sides. Down we came toward the mad waves in a swift glide. In sudden apprehension, I dropped my hand on his shoulder.

"Man, you can't land in a sea like that! It's suicide!"

Without a word, he shook off my hand and continued our steep glide toward the rock. I drew my breath in apprehension of a crash.

I do not blame Charlie for what happened. He is as skilful a pilot as I know. It was a mad freak of the sea that did the thing.

The gray waste of mountainous, white-crested waves rose swiftly up to meet us, with the rock with the girl clinging to it just to our right. The *Golden Gull* struck the crest of a wave, buried herself in the foam, and plunged down the long slope to the trough. We rose safely to the crest of the oncoming roller, and I saw the black outline of the rock not a dozen yards away.

Charlie had landed with all his skill. It was not his fault that the blustering wind caught the ship as she reached the crest of the wave and flung her sidewise toward the rock. It is no fault of his that the white-capped mountain of racing green water completed what the wind had begun and hurled the frail plane crashing on the rock.

I have a confused memory of the wild plunge at the mercy of the wave, of my despair as I realized that we were being wrecked. I must have been knocked unconscious when we struck. The next I remember I was opening my eyes to find myself on the rock, Charlie's strong arm on my shoulder. I was soaked with icy brine and my head was aching from a heavy blow.

Virginia, shivering and blue, was perched beside us. I could see no sign of the plane: the mighty sea had swept away what was left of it. Clinging to the lee side of the rock I saw the black tentacles of the giant octopus—waiting for a wave to dash us to its mercy.

"All right, Hammond?" Charlie inquired anxiously. "I'm afraid you got a pretty nasty bump on the head. About all I could do to fish you out before the *Gull* was swept away."

He helped me to a better position to withstand the force of the great roller that came plunging down upon us like a moving mountain. Virginia was in his arms, too exhausted to do more than cling to him.

"What can we do?" I said, shaking water from my head.

"Not a thing. We're in a pretty bad fix, I imagine. In a few seconds we will feel the attraction of the meteor's field— the force with which I tried to draw Virginia to the crater through the fourth dimension. I don't know what will happen; we may be jerked out of space altogether. And if that doesn't get us, the tide and the octopus will..."

His voice was drowned in the roar of the coming wave. A mountain of water deluged us. Half drowned, I clung to the rock against the mad water.

Then blinding blue light flashed about me. A sharp crash rang in my ears, like splintering glass. I reeled, and felt myself falling headlong.

I brought up on soft sand.

I sat up, dumbfounded, and opened my eyes. I was sitting on the steep sandy tide of a conical pit. Charlie and Virginia were sprawled beside me, looking as astonished as I felt. Charlie got to his knees and lifted the limp form of the girl in his arms.

Something snapped in my brain. The sand-walled pit was suddenly familiar. I got to my feet and clambered out of it. I saw that we were on our own landing field.

Astonishingly, we were back in the meteor crater. Charlie's vanished apparatus was scattered about us. I saw the gray side of the rough iron meteorite itself, half-buried in the sand at the bottom of the pit.

"What—what happened?" I demanded of Charlie.

"Don't you see? Simple enough. I should have thought of it before. The field of the meteorite brought Virginia— and us—through to this point in space. But it could not bring us back through time; instead, the apparatus itself was jerked forward through time. That is why it vanished. We got here just twelve hours and forty minutes after I closed the switch, since we had been looking that far into the future. The mathematical explanation—"

"That's enough for me," I said hastily. "We better see about a warm, dry bed for Virginia, and some hot soup or something."

Now the rough gray meteorite, in a neat glass case, rests above the mantel in the library of a beautiful home where I am a frequent guest. I was there one evening, a few days ago, when Charlie King fell silent in one of his fits of mathematical speculation.

"Einstein again?" I chaffingly inquired.

He raised his brown eyes and looked at me. "Hammond, since relativity enabled us to find the Meteor Girl, you ought to be convinced."

Virginia—whom her husband calls the Meteor Girl—came laughingly to the rescue.

"Yes, Mr. Hammond, what do you think of Einstein now?"

## THE END

# Tyrants Need To Be Loved

## By MURRAY LEINSTER

*Everyone want to be loved...but how far is are you willing to go?*

DOCTOR ZOCH had said that nobody wants to be loved as much as a tyrant, because to be all-powerful is to live in constant fear. But tonight Igor felt no love at all for the Ruler. He felt a sickening terror, which he tried to turn into fury for the sake of courage. But it did not work for him.

All of Diane's moons were below the horizon, and the night was pitch-dark, but there was light ahead and his teeth tended to chatter. The light was that rectangular lane of pitiless glare, which was the fence about the prison camp. Doctor Zoch was a prisoner in it. Already Igor could see the fence itself—woven barbed wire—and the guard towers—raised on stilt-like metal legs—and he imagined that he could see in the center that huddle of noisesomeness, which was the barracks for the prisoners condemned to hard labor on one-fourth rations until they died.

He halted and looked at his companions. Like himself they wore dark clothing, with dark masks and thick dark gloves. Two of them carried stunners—bulky, hand-made objects good for three hundred yards. Two others carried spidery, insulated aluminum ladders. Igor carried other handmade pocket stunners—they had been developed at the Institute and discreetly kept secret—and a flask for Doctor Zoch if the impossible happened and they got him out of the prison camp.

"We're getting too close," said Igor, in a tone that surprised him by its steadiness. "We crawl from here."

Teeth chattered for answer.

The five of them went down on their hands and knees. They crawled forward. There was only silence everywhere in the night. Now again a searchlight on a guard tower flicked to brightness. Its beam wandered lazily and erratically over the enclosure and the hovels at its center. Then it winked out. It did not search the outside darkness.

They crawled interminably. Igor kept his teeth tightly clamped shut. Doctor Zoch had said that the Ruler, as a tyrant, wanted desperately to be beloved by his people. This event followed from that statement. Doctor Zoch had designed a machine, to be built in the shops of the Parapsychological Institute. He had begun to build it and it was almost finished. But he had reported it and its theory to Research Supervision, and he'd been arrested in consequence. Now Igor and the others had been commanded to finish the job Doctor Zoch could not complete because of his arrest. Obviously, the police could not release him without admitting that they'd made a mistake. But the Ruler wanted the Machine. If it worked, it would make him as much beloved as any tyrant could desire. It would give him control over even the imagination of his subjects. So Igor and the others had been commanded to complete the Machine that Doctor Zoch designed. It would be fatal to know its workings after it was done, so they needed Doctor Zoch.

One of the crawling figures made a sound. All five stopped. Igor said in the lowest of tones:

"Take your time, but don't pull the trigger until you're both ready. Then say so and pull the trigger. We don't want to waste a second."

There were no stunners anywhere but these. The big ones wavered and steadied. The signal came. Igor and the others leaped to their feet and rushed for the charged barbed-wire fence. They rushed toward the light. They could be seen from two of the watchtowers. There should have come a stabbing, flickering burst of machine-gun fire. They should have fallen, while other guns leisurely pumped more bullets into them. Flares should have leaped up, illuminating everything.

But nothing happened. And there was no alarm. Panting, they reached the fence under a tower. In the dark space they set up a ladder. One climbed swiftly and set up the other ladder on the inside. He half-slid to the ground within. The others followed swiftly. All three raced across the brightly-lit area inside the line of electrified fence. They reached the darkness of the massed, matted, filthy buildings, which were the shelters for persons suspected of unkind thoughts about the Ruler.

They vanished. And then it was as if the guards returned to duty. A searchlight turned on. It swept along the crazy, unsanitary shacks containing the prisoners. From those shacks smells came out to contaminate the night. From them came moanings of men in exhausted sleep. The searchlight beam flickered back. It went out.

Igor was sickened, inside the barracks. The three of them, of course, turned on their pocket-sized stunners. No prisoner stirred. Because of the stunners they were unaware of them or anything else for the time being—which was good fortune for the prisoners. The three intruders searched fiercely. They found Doctor Zoch, and the sight of him roused fury.

Igor gave the signal, a flicker of light in one of the barracks windows. The three of them went out, half-carrying Doctor Zoch. They rushed him across the brightly lighted ground. One of them swarmed up the ladder. The others passed Doctor Zoch up to him. They got him down on the other side and hurried away toward the outer blackness. The last man followed, carrying both the ladders.

There was no alarm. Presently, a searchlight flicked on in one of the guard towers. It wavered lazily here and there, lighting the walls of the hovels in which the prisoners remained at night, so long as they continued to live.

The two men who'd used the big stunners crawled away. When far enough from the guard towers, they also got up and ran, panting, for the waiting car. Incredibly, everything had gone according to schedule. They were still alive. Doctor Zoch was free. There was no suspicion of his escape. The whole thing had been managed because of the stunners. They had made the stunners within the past four days—since Doctor Zoch's arrest—because the Ruler wanted the Machine, and they were afraid to complete it without Doctor Zoch's specific advice.

They were afraid the Machine would operate as expected.

On one hemisphere of the planet Diane the Ruler reigned without limit to his power. On the other half, things were more satisfactory. But under the Ruler there was terror everywhere. The Ruler himself was afraid, because very many people wished very desperately to be rid of him because he had secret police and prison camps and used them mercilessly against his opponents. But he had to have them because people wanted desperately to be rid of him. He knew there were plots against him. He suspected there were more than his secret police discovered. There were times when he wished bitterly that he were beloved by his people. It would be very good indeed to stop being afraid.

It seemed that the Institute was near when they were only minutes from the prison camp. As they entered the city, Igor held the flask to Doctor Zoch's mouth. The old man was pitiably weak, but he tried to protest the risk that had been taken for his rescue.

"Hush!" said Igor gently, "drink this. It is milk and eggs and good brandy. We have more troubles ahead. Drink, for strength."

"But it is madness!" protested Doctor Zoch. "I am only one man. I would not have lived long. It was madness to risk so much for me. You could not have feared that I would speak..."

Igor tilted the flask. Doctor Zoch drank. Igor felt very strange, very much, he considered, as one would feel when he had newly died. What was past was irretrievable. Nothing could matter any more. The worst had happened. From now on there could be only tranquility or purest horror. One could only wait to find out which.

The car threaded streets. It braked and stopped in darkness. Three of them slipped out like eels. They lifted Doctor Zoch to the ground. The car sped away. Trezk drove it. He took a very desperate chance, did Trezk. He would go back to his tiny house and put into the petrol-tank the exact amount of fuel this night's work had used up. Then he'd burn the plastic bags the fuel had been in, and drink heavily of brandy so he would be convincingly stupefied if the police came to his house in the morning. Drake would be far away by daylight. He'd have disposed of the ladders and masks and gloves beyond any imaginable search.

But Lechy and Igor and Sohn hustled Doctor Zoch through a garden gate. It was pitch-dark. They went ten feet. Twenty. Thirty. They stopped, and Igor bent down and heaved. A flagstone lifted. They descended swiftly, all but Sohn, who remained behind to make absolutely sure that the flagstone would show no sign of having been disturbed when morning came. When that was attended to he would turn up in a disreputable place, seemingly very drunk and in no condition to have taken part in any conspiracy. The flagstone had been arranged two years before, when Igor discovered the drain going from the Institute to nowhere. It was an old drain, three feet in diameter, and before the Institute was built it had doubtless served some purpose for the buildings then occupying the Institute's site. Now it was a bolthole, with its flagstoned exit outside a house that Kett—since dead—had rented on pretense that he meant to throw improper parties in it.

Igor marveled at their forethought as he tucked Doctor Zoch in the makeshift subway vehicle they had built in the Institute's shops. When they prepared this, they'd had no real idea that to be a member of the staff would ever constitute a deadly danger. Then they'd been under the Ruler's direct protection. They'd devised the highly convincing demonstration of an appalling weapon that was then needed to avert a war the Ruler couldn't have won. Enemy spies must have found out since that it was a fake, but the Ruler'd gained time to seat himself firmly in power and build up military might nobody wanted to challenge. The Ruler had thought well of the Institute in those good old days. Nowdays. Now... Well, now things were quite different.

"Just lie quiet," said Igor almost humorously, in the inky and ill-smelling darkness underneath the flagstone. "We will have you home in minutes."

The vehicle moved swiftly through the drain with its three passengers. It ran almost four hundred yards, beneath two streets with policemen on them, and under the line of sentries about the Institute. It rolled silently past the appliance room and into a spare tank that nobody could imagine was the terminus of a railroad built without the knowledge of the Ruler's spies. Nobody would suspect anything like this!

Igor checked for presences outside. He opened the tank's manhole, which seemed so firmly bolted shut. He wriggled out and helped Doctor Zoch while Lechy boosted. He got the old man to the floor. Lechy scrambled out of the tank. Igor said:

"The manhole, Lechy."

"Ridiculous!" said Doctor Zoch, reproachfully. "This is the Institute! You have brought me back here? It is suicide! But it was also suicide to come after me. Why did you, Igor?"

"We need you," said Igor. "The Ruler wants the Machine you designed. But he does not want anybody who could design another to be left alive. So he ordered your murder. When the Machine is finished, he will not want anybody able to duplicate it to be left alive. So he will have us killed. Yet if we fail we will be killed for failure. So we need you to tell us what to do."

"I fear," said Doctor Zoch very sadly, "that all my plan is spoiled. I will be discovered here."

"No," said Igor grimly. "There are sentries all about, inside and outside the building. But we have stunners. We made them from your first test of the principles of the Machine. So, though nobody could have left the building undiscovered, we did. Nobody could have taken you from the prison camp. But we did. Certainly no one could bring you here and hide you successfully. But we will. Lechy?"

He pulled out a pocket stunner—it was crudity itself, to look at it—and nodded to Lechy. The stunners had made everything possible. Doctor Zoch had tested the Machine's theory by such an improvisation. He'd proved that those odd-shaped waves, which produced the experience of consciousness, could be inhibited. Then he went on to design the Machine to enhance them selectively. But the stunners were the essential first steps. The Machine would be a powerful stimulator of certain groups of waves. The stunner prevented them. The Machine would produce certain experiences in all the brains within its range. The stunners prevented any experiences at all.

Lechy went up the stairway from the basement. Moving silently, he peered out. He signaled one sentry in the hall above. He aimed a pocket stunner. He went out the door.

Igor helped Doctor Zoch begin the climb. He almost carried the old man. He tried not to notice the bloody places on Doctor Zoch's face. He did note that touching certain spots made Doctor Zoch wince. Probably broken bones gotten when he was arrested, though he'd offered no resistance. But they might have been broken when he was first beaten to make him confess treason to the Ruler. No sensible man would confess, of course. If one denied everything convincingly, there was a chance that the secret police would end it quickly. Of course, they would never release one. That would be to admit that they'd been mistaken. Nobody could admit to a mistake in the Ruler's service!

Doctor Zoch was pitiably frail. Igor felt an almost maternal yearning over his feebleness as they climbed the stairway. They reached the upper hall. There was a sentry there, uniformed and armed. But Lechy held a stunner on him. His consciousness was suspended. He did not fall, but he did not see or hear or feel or know anything. When the stunner-beam went off, he would not know that he had momentarily ceased to know anything. He looked perfectly natural, even now. But his eyes were blank.

Igor helped Doctor Zoch across the hall under the very nose of the sentry who had no awareness of anything, not even of his lack of awareness. They went through the door beyond the hall. Lechy backed into it, holding the stunner steady. He closed the door and flicked off the stunner. He listened, and mopped his forehead. Only a very few seconds later Igor helped Doctor Zoch to a chair. They had reached his own private quarters in the Institute's main building.

"Now," said Igor, "we bandage you and tape you where needful. I think you should rest. Then we can get to business."

"I do not need rest," said Doctor Zoch faintly. "I had too much pain to sleep, but they did not exhaust me, I would have died too soon. But I insist that it was not wise to bring me here."

"Hush," said Igor gently. "I will let you talk presently. First let me wash off this blood. And you have broken ribs, haven't you? Hmm... Your hand... Your..."

Despite himself his voice changed. But Doctor Zoch did not notice. He went suddenly into the deep, deep sleep of weakness and exhaustion.

Over the hemisphere under the Ruler, parents went anxiously over the homework papers of their children, lest there be some incautious statement implying less than blind admiration of the Ruler and the State. Children were graded for loyalty. It was an indication of parental attitudes, too. Loyal students never failed of good marks. On graduation, they got the good jobs the State employment offices had to pass out. It was essential that one's children get good grades in loyalty! And loyalty also involved slavish respect for any governmental functionary who wore a uniform.

But the Ruler was not satisfied. Before he could feel really secure he must have the inner loyalty of his subjects, too. To be safe against assassination, he needed to be loved by his people.

As of now, he wasn't.

It was a full general who came to the Institute next day. He arrived as Igor stood before the incomplete Machine with an expression of helplessness on his face. He straightened to attention at sight of the general. The general beamed at him.

"I am General Tilsit," he explained. "Research Supervision. I have been assigned to the special supervision of the making of the Machine."

"Ah, yes," said Igor respectfully. "I am apprehensive about the Machine. It is so completely the design of Doctor Zoch and the theory is so complex that it is frightening to try to complete it."

There was silence. Doctor Zoch had been arrested five days before. Officially, the rest was silence. One did not inquire about a person who had been arrested. One did not even ask questions if the police took one's wife or daughter into custody. There was the splendor of the State to contemplate. The Ruler had decreed that no personal sorrow should diminish one's rejoicing in the magnificence of the State. He did not put it that way, but people bitterly understood him to mean that it should make up for murder and brutality, and the madness taught in the public schools, and every foulness practiced by everybody who could wangle a uniformed State position.

The general tapped a cigarette delicately on his wrist. "You do not despair of success?" he asked.

"Oh, no," said Igor quickly. "The Ruler himself—" and he wondered ironically if he'd seemed to capitalize the pronoun— "the Ruler himself ordered the work done. Of course, I shall accomplish anything the Ruler commands me to."

"Except," said General Tilsit, "that he might order an impossibility."

Igor made his face go blank. General Tilsit was talking pure treason. Nobody should admit to any thought that the Ruler might make a mistake. But Research Supervision officials were privileged. They were even ordered to talk treason on occasion. They had trapped many people that way. Kett, poor devil, was one of them. But he'd managed to make the soldiers kill him when they came for his arrest. Igor was not to be tricked so easily.

"I am sorry, sir," he said stiffly, "but I cannot agree that the Ruler could be in error."

The general lighted his cigarette. Igor knew that he was aware of Doctor Zoch's disappearance from a slave labor camp, and that he would pounce if Igor showed that he knew it, too.

"Tell me about the Machine," ordered the general abruptly.

Igor took a deep breath.

"It has been found," he said carefully, "that there is a complex substance in the brain, which breaks down in different ways. The result of each breakdown is the experience of emotion. One way of breakdown produces fear. Others yield other emotional experiences—anger, grief, love, and so on."

The general frowned.

"Well?"

"The Machine," said Igor, "broadcasts waveforms, which cause the breakdown of that substance in different ways. In effect, the Machine broadcasts emotions. Anyone within its range will feel whatever emotion the operator desires, the kind of emotion being determined by the waveform, and its intensity by the frequency. Therefore, it can be modulated and the emotions of an entire population can be made simultaneous. Of course, they will be associated with simultaneous stimuli."

The general looked puzzled. He wasn't. He'd heard all this before. He'd been briefed. But he would trap Igor if he could.

"And what possible use would that be?" he demanded.

Igor said with a fine air of sincerity:

"No intelligent man could oppose the Ruler, sir. But there are stupid ones with emotional associations, which lead them to do so. The Ruler himself has mentioned dissidents. His plans for the State and for his people are hampered by individuals who are emotionally driven to oppose him and harm the State. With the Machine, the Ruler can make a speech with everyone in the nation listening, and with the Machine broadcasting the emotions intelligent men already feel when they hear the Ruler speak."

The general regarded Igor out of the corners of his eyes. He hesitated, then spoke.

"What then?"

"Why," said Igor earnestly, "if the Ruler speaks of his enemies, and all his hearers experience overwhelming anger, an association is formed, a conditioning association. Afterward no one will be able even to think of the Ruler's enemies without anger. If the Ruler speaks of his love and care for his people, and they feel overwhelming love as they listen, they will be unable to think of him without experiencing a surge of affection. So everybody will become unanimous in loyalty to him. Everyone will be what the Ruler wishes each of us to be. Everyone will be loyal to the Ruler, even the stupid ones who are now emotionally disturbed."

He hoped that no trace of irony had crept into his voice.

"Pavlov's dogs, eh?" said the general drily.

"It is not the same thing at all, sir," protested Igor instantly. "That ancient process had no purpose. But this—this is a way to bring every person in the nation into complete accord with the State. It will remove the seeds of crime. It will make treason unthinkable."

He seemed tense. He was. The general regarded him sardonically.

"Very well. You are convincing. But there will be no work done on the Machine without a Research Supervision general officer present. The Machine will be guarded night and day. No doubt this is it. Now, exactly how does it, or will it operate?"

Igor explained the theory and the process. The general listened noncommittally. When he left, Igor's clothing felt clammy from the cold sweat that had poured out on his skin. His life had hung in the balance with every word of his explanation.

The Ruler found the strain excessive. He sent a Cabinet Officer to a prison camp and had an army colonel shot. Their loyalty had become doubtful, which could be a prelude to conspiracy. He was bitter because he could not fully trust anybody. Those around him were opportunists, seeking greatness and riches through him. They'd betrayed him in an instant... He wished that there was someone he could trust. Even the people would be a protection against conspirators. If they could be persuaded to love him as subjects should love their Ruler, he would have less reason to be afraid...

Igor closed the door of his private quarters. As usual, after a session of work upon the Machine with a Research Supervision general officer glaring at him, and a dozen sentries with loaded rifles in the room, he was nerve-racked but he tried to speak casually to Doctor Zoch.

"You may be pleased to hear," he observed, "that you are dead."

Doctor Zoch said mildly:

"How did I die?"

"You crept from your barrack," Igor told him, "and crawled into the camp crematory. There you cut your throat. When the morgue wagon came around with the bodies of prisoners who had died during the night, they simply dumped the other bodies on top of yours. All were disposed of together. The prison camp officials were very pleased to find a prisoner to whom you had confided your intention. They would have been in a nice fix if the Ruler ordered you questioned again, and they could not find you..."

"Poor devil," said Doctor Zoch sadly. "I hope the guards gave him a loaf of bread. The prisoner would have invented that story in hope of such a reward."

Igor moved restlessly. His nerves were taut and jangling.

"The Machine is nearly finished," he said abruptly. "It could be used at low power tomorrow. You must tell me what to do."

Doctor Zoch said gently,

"You must finish it. Properly. It must work as I said it would."

"Why?" demanded Igor.

"Because," said Doctor Zoch in the same tone, "it has to pass tests. It would not be used at full scale and full power unless it had been proved to work without defect. It is to be used to make the Ruler beloved and his enemies hated. Do you think he will risk that it work backwards if at all?"

Igor ground his teeth.

"Then it must work exactly as you promised."

"Exactly," said Doctor Zoch mildly.

"It has to be capable of turning everyone within its range into a zombie, a robot, a slave so degraded that he wishes nothing more than to be a slave!"

"In theory that should be its effect," agreed Doctor Zoch. "I designed it. There is no other way to bring about what must happen, unless by bloody war. But I am not a traitor to you, Igor, nor to my fellow sub-citizens."

Igor said irresolutely,

"Will you tell me the trick—the secret part of the device that will make it—make it weaken the Ruler's power? You must have designed it for something like that..."

Doctor Zoch made a movement as if to put the tips of his fingers together in a well remembered gesture. But one of his hands was heavily bandaged. There were broken bones in it. He shrugged and peered at Igor.

"I will not even say that it will weaken the power of the Ruler. I will say nothing that could be extracted from you under torture." His tone was firm. It was almost brisk.

Igor stared at him. Then he said desperately:

"Then I will finish it. But if the Machine is to subdue all Diane to the Ruler, with other worlds after it, so that tyrants turn humanity into a race of slaves... If that is to happen, you will have to hide very deep in hell to escape the dead who will hunt you through all eternity!"

Doctor Zoch looked somberly after him as he turned away.

The Ruler moved restlessly about his palace. His secret police were on the trail of conspirators who seemed to be linked to persons in his very palace. But some of those hinted at had been so loyal for so long that the Ruler darkly suspected the secret police of trying to remove everybody who would serve him loyally, so they alone could control the State. But he could not be sure… He did not know who was loyal and who was not.

Cautiously, he considered the Machine now under construction, at the Parapsychological Institute. Its former head, one Doctor Zoch, had respectfully proposed it as a way by which everybody—everybody!—could be conditioned to perfect loyalty to the Ruler, and bitter hatred of his enemies. The Ruler had disposed of Doctor Zoch because he was dangerous. But the machine—if it could be made—if all his people could be conditioned to impassioned, emotional loyalty. If all his subjects could be made forcibly into his adorers…

He struck a gong. He ordered a report on the progress of the Machine.

General Tilsit sardonically supervised the small-scale test. Troop-carrier loads of prisoners from jails and prison camps arrived by night at the Parapsychological Institute. They were not only handcuffed but chained to each other, and Igor gagged at the smell of degradation when they shuffled into the lecture hall of the Institute. Some were sunk in apathy so complete that they were like automatons. But some were bright-eyed scarecrows who defied torture and death and spat at him and at the general as they passed.

Guards herded them into place. They filled half the hall, intended for sedate and learned lectures on aspects of the physical nature of consciousness. General Tilsit regarded them sardonically. He nodded to Igor, and he approached the Machine. There was a screen on which the Ruler's more-than-life-size image would presently appear. There were speaker-units to give out his recorded voice. And there was the Machine.

Igor took his place at the controls.

"You are quite ready?" asked the general. "All is in order?"

"Yes, general," said Igor nervously. "I believe everything is as Doctor Zoch designed it. I have tested everything. But I am nervous. Naturally…"

A squalling minor uproar came from the prisoners. Some of them guessed that a novel and deadly weapon was to be tested on them. They snarled at the guards, at Igor, at everything.

"The Machine's waves," said the general, "the ones that create emotions. They will not go through the walls?"

"No," said Igor. "The walls are metal foil."

"And you and I, will we be affected like the prisoners?"

Igor pointed to a woven copper cage, which almost surrounded the Machine. Its open side was toward the prisoners.

"The waves cannot pass that screen," he explained. "They will strike only the prisoners. They are not reflected."

"Proceed," said the general. Matter-of-factly he drew a weapon and held it bearing negligently upon Igor. It was, of course, a precaution.

Igor threw a switch. The image of the Ruler appeared on the screen. His deep-sunk eyes seemed to gaze at the chained prisoners, whose degradation was a consequence of his rule. The uproar multiplied. Snarls and catcalls, screamed imprecations and shrieks pleading innocence, all mingled with hissings and oaths to make an horrific din. Some of these men had nothing left to fear, not even the Ruler. They cursed him defiantly.

Then, the Ruler's voice boomed out from the speakers. Igor reflected bitterly that the Institute had designed that recorded voice, and the microphone and amplifiers, which made it resonant and fatherly and splendidly masculine. The prisoners howled at it.

Then Igor touched the first emotional control on the Machine. Its function was to produce the emotion of awe.

It did.

The record of image and speech, together, lasted half an hour. It was one of the Ruler's shorter speeches. Igor had a typescript of it, with cues for the operation of the Machine to synchronize violent, appropriate emotions with every word. He felt extraordinary personal sensations as he swayed and ruled the poor devils who were the guinea pigs for this test.

When the Ruler's voice died away and his image faded from the screen, the prisoners were changed. They were fanatics. They had roared in ardent echoing of his defiance of foreign enemies. They had wept when he spoke of his sorrow that he needed to ask sacrifices of his people. They shouted crazy, adoring assurances when he begged his people for their loyalty. And the emaciated, half-starved, doomed victims of his rule snarled with rage when he spoke of those who hated and opposed and would depose him.

When the thing was ended, General Tilsit was very pale.

"I walked beyond the copper cage," he told Igor. "I felt the emotions I saw you impose. The thing is astounding! The State the Ruler has founded will last for a thousand years!" He added, "I shall increase the guard over the machine. Hold yourself ready to operate it when the Ruler shall command. There, must be no fumbling. The matter is too important."

Igor swallowed. The guards herded the prisoners back into the courtyard of the Institute and into the troop carriers, which had brought them. They shambled as they walked. Some staggered from weakness. But they babbled to each other with a pathetic enthusiasm of the Ruler and their love for him. On the way back to the prisons where they would die within weeks or days, they piped up feebly, singing in praise of the Ruler.

The demonstration was conclusive. The Ruler heard the report of it, and brooded, and twice made gestures toward the arrest and execution not only of Igor, but of General Tilsit as well. The Machine was very dangerous. But if it were used...

The Ruler proclaimed a great occasion. He would make an address to all his people. He would make announcements of an unparalleled kind. He might even grant amnesty to some offenders. He would show his benevolence to all his people and every man and woman and child must see and hear him on penalty of being considered a traitor.

The population of one whole hemisphere of the planet Diane prepared to obey. The Ruler's speeches did not mean much. There had been too many of them. But nobody wanted the secret police to suspect he hadn't listened.

The sun shone brightly, and white clouds floated in the sky—which was blue as on all human-occupied planets—and there was self-evident preparation by nature itself for so important a matter as a speech by the Ruler. All business stopped. Every store and office closed. There were no schools. All traffic suspended so passengers could stand before one of the great screens set up even in villages for passersby to watch. There were no picnics, secret-police floaters made sure of that! Nobody in the Ruler's domain seriously considered any other activity than seeing and hearing—and being seen to be doing so—while the Ruler's address was in progress.

He spoke from the head of the great white-stone stairway that led up from the Avenue of the State to his palace. The stairs were three hundred feet wide. The columns of the palace portico loomed above them. Flags and banners floated bravely in the sunshine. Tens of thousands of inhabitants of his capital city thronged to see him in person—at whatever distance—and there was not an inch of ground space or on nearby roofs that was not colored by the garments of his subjects. Loudspeakers were everywhere to repeat his words. All over the hemisphere all other activity stopped while the Ruler spoke.

Magnificent, blaring trumpets sounded. Then drums beat, and the trumpets sounded again.

Then the Ruler appeared on the great stairway before his palace. He was surrounded by his guards and officials, of course, but he appeared convincingly in the midst of his beloved people. They crowded the lower steps within tens of yards of him. He raised his hand gravely, and a roar of sharply supervised applause replied.

(In the Institute, watching a television monitor for his cues and with a script of the Ruler's speech before him for guidance, Igor pressed the first button on the Machine's control board. It was the button for awe.)

The roar of greeting ceased, and the people of the Ruler, as if involuntarily, bowed down before him. ("Splendid!" said General Tilsit, with a weapon pointing negligently at Igor's body.)

The Ruler spoke, and for a long minute there was a deep and astonishing silence while his words rolled out of many resonant loudspeakers. There was no one before the palace—nor before any of the screens, which gave even clearer pictures of the Ruler all over his domain—who did not listen with a feeling of astonished admiration to his beginning. Then there came a feeling of ecstatic joy as he spoke of his love for his people. They cheered, vast volumes of sound before his palace; thin and reedy shouts before the screens in tiny villages. He touched upon his unremitting labor for the welfare of his subjects. An enormous feeling of affection overwhelmed his audience over an entire hemisphere. They shouted again.

(The monitor swept over the crowds, and Igor in the Institute saw rapt and eager faces, flushed and suffused with emotion. He glanced at the script and prepared to rouse frenzied hatred of the Ruler's enemies when they were mentioned. He did. The image on the monitor showed the Ruler's face close-up, and it was triumphant and hungry and eager. It had been a long time since the Ruler could believe in the total sincerity of all who listened to him. Now he knew it again. He had the feel of his audience. It loved him. It adored him!)

The Ruler spoke of those traitors and dissidents who had wished him ill, and the crowd uttered a roaring growl. Had any man present been named as his enemy, the mob would have torn him to bits. But the Ruler assured his people that such folk were very few. They bellowed their joy. He promised them that he would continue to serve them without remission, without respite, without rest, and with unfailing love. And a booming, screaming tumult of hysterical adulation answered.

(General Tilsit put aside his weapon and said with an amazement that was not in the least sardonic: "Think of it... This is happening all over the nation... Everywhere!")

Igor compressed his lips. He followed the script of the Ruler's speech with conscientious exactitude. But a cold sensation ran up and down his spine. The Machine did all that it was supposed to do.

The monitor showed other crowds in other cities, in transports of emotion, which followed exactly the buttons that Igor pressed. Everywhere there was a tumult of loyalty and love for the Ruler, which urgently needed expression, but could only be shown by cries and swayings so long as his figure stayed on the screens and his voice came out of loudspeakers. Never before had any man been adored as the Ruler was. The blood drained from Igor's cheeks. From this moment on, his people would worship the Ruler blindly. They would enslave themselves joyfully to him. They would perform anything he might command. And this insane conditioning was permanent. It would last. They would never be released from it!

Igor numbly pressed down the button to arouse extravagances of affection, appropriate to the conclusion of the Ruler's speech. He held it down. He saw even the guards about the Ruler turn to regard him with warmly shining eyes. He saw the Ruler's generals shouting incoherently of their love for him. They crowded about him to swear undying fealty. Igor saw a vast, slow, irresistible movement of the crowds in the streets.

Shouting, screaming, stumbling and rising, with open mouths babbling of love and loyalty and rejoicing, the Ruler's listeners moved to protest their impassioned affection from the nearest possible position. The guards crowded about him, shouting joyously.

Igor was still dazed when he faced Doctor Zoch in his quarters, after it was all over. He'd been unable to talk to the older man. He was partly ashamed and partly exultant and wholly confused. He stammered out some words.

"No, Igor," said Doctor Zoch mildly. "I did not expect what happened. I expected something, of course. I knew the Ruler would make a speech telling his people how he loved them, and how passionately he wished everybody to be happy and free of fear and hunger and sadness. I knew he would tell them—and the Machine would condition them so they had to believe—that he desired nothing but their happiness and their love. The Machine would make them believe every syllable. This much I expected. I even expected his government to fall apart before he was half through his speech, and it did. But I did not expect what took place where he was."

Igor paced back and forth. There were no sentries anywhere about the Institute, now. Tacitly, but openly, Doctor Zoch was again the Institute's head. There were other pleasing changes in the state of things on this hemisphere.

"But I don't understand," protested Igor. "You must have panned…"

Doctor Zoch nodded his head comfortably.

"I planned to invoke a natural law," he said gently. "The Ruler wished his people to think him kind and gentle and wise and benevolent. So I designed a machine to produce such emotions as would condition them so they could think nothing else. And when the Machine was used, the law of nature operated. As soon as he finished his speech, and while the television screens showed his generals cheering him and the people moving toward him, weeping with joy and love—why— in other cities the people began to massacre the secret police because the Ruler did not want anybody to act as they did, and to tear down the prison camps because he did not want anyone oppressed or sad or hungry or in fear. The Ruler had said he disapproved of very nearly every agency of his rule, though not by name. So the people, out of love for him, destroyed what he disapproved of. It was a perfectly natural thing. It is a natural law that we try to do what is wished by people we love..."

Igor swallowed. Doctor Zoch said regretfully: "But it is sad about the people on the palace steps. I do not think of the Ruler, but—how many were killed there?"

Igor did not answer. He felt horrible. He'd sat at the controls of the machine, his finger frozen on the button that called up extravagant love, when he realized what must happen. He couldn't take it away. In the monitor he saw the crowd surging forward, shouting happily, pressing to get closer to the Ruler they now loved beyond imagination. They were irresistibly impelled to move toward him to tell him nearby of their feelings of loyalty, of their resolve to be his perfect subjects. They stumbled in their haste. They did not think. Faces shining, they crowded closer and closer...

Igor did not like to remember what the monitors had shown him while he sat at the controls of the Machine. The cameraman there must have been frozen as Igor was, too much stunned by horror to turn his camera away. So Igor had seen every bit of the tragedy—though mercifully from a distance—as the crowd swept up the palace steps, cheering, and crowded about the Ruler's cheering guards, and was pushed on terribly from behind so that nobody could stop. Nobody.

More than a hundred of the crowd had been crushed to death in their attempt to tell the Ruler of their love. That was not the whole list, of course. The whole list included nearly every one of the Ruler's guards, and all his generals.

The Ruler could only be recognized by his decorations. The rest of him was trampled past any possible recognition.

## THE END

# Death Sentence

## By CHESTER S. GEIER

*They were just rabbits in a cage, but their death sentence meant a lot more than was apparent on the surface.*

I HAD something of the feeling of godhood as I stood there beside the control board, waiting for Professor Weller's signal. For in my hands was the power of life and death. Of course, it was only over two scrawny, flop-eared rabbits, but I knew that the vibrator—even in model form—was deadly enough to kill human beings.

Death was there in the laboratory—waiting, just as I was waiting. Of the two of us, Death, I'm sure, was the most patient, I was anxious to have done with this evening's business, anxious to get out of the laboratory and keep my date with Gail...

Professor Weller was talking, explaining how his invention worked. He waved his plump hands animatedly, and his round, ruddy face shone with triumph.

The three men listened...

Major William Calhern looked cold and suspicious. If his sole job was interviewing men like Professor Weller, I didn't blame him for looking that way. Major Calhern had been sent from Washington by the war department to investigate the potentialities of the vibrator as a war weapon. He looked thin and hard, and somehow his uniform seemed just a bit too large for him.

Professor John Arndt looked disgusted. He hated war, and suffering, and death, and I knew that he hated the vibrator, hated Professor Weller for taking delight in explaining what the deadly thing could do...

Norman Hollis looked sullen. Occasionally he glanced at me, and I avoided his eyes. He was Gail's father, and I knew he was blaming me for my part in this, however slight it was. Norman Hollis was an inventor, too. The vibrator had been developed from an idea of his, and doubtless he felt that he had been robbed.

"...ultra high-frequency vibrations," Professor Weller was saying. "You've heard how a certain harp or violin note will shatter a thin glass goblet. Well, my invention utilizes the same principle, though on an infinitely greater scale. The vibrator, in fact, can cause glass to become dust, can pulverize brick and stone, and can weaken many metals."

Major Calhern asked, "Does your invention act also on human beings?"

WELLER nodded his white head vigorously. "It kills them—by destroying the delicate tissues of the brain. I will give a demonstration in a moment. First, notice that enclosure. It is soundproof, and so we may watch the proceedings quite in safety." He pointed at a great enclosed cage in one corner of the room. It had very thick walls, and the glass viewing plate set in the front was also thick. Within the enclosure sat the two rabbits, wriggling their pink noses. Some three feet above them, suspended from the roof of the enclosure, was the model vibrator.

Weller looked at Major Calhern. "Now for the demonstration. Try to imagine those two rabbits as human beings. All right, Kirk, go ahead."

This last was to me. Feeling like an executioner, I adjusted a couple of dials on the control board, then threw in a switch. I'd seen it happen before, but now I stared fascinatedly through the glass viewing plate of the enclosure.

The two rabbits started as the first vibrations hit them. Their ears jerked up, and they took a few hopping steps.

Then they keeled over and lay still, and I knew they were dead.

It was as simple and unmelodramatic as that. The most deadly and efficient forms of death often strike that way.

The three men were silent, as though awed by what they had witnessed. Major Calhern no longer seemed cold and suspicious. His lean, hard face looked convinced—and even admiring. But Professor John Arndt's disgust had increased, as had Norman Hollis' sullenness.

Beaming like a showman who has put on an excellent performance, Weller walked over to the soundproof enclosure and unlocked a door in its side. First he removed the vibrator from its supports, setting the device on a workbench. Then he pulled out the dead rabbits, laying them upon a table for examination.

Major Calhern was the only one who bothered to look them over. He did so with quick, deft movements of his thin, long-fingered hands. Then he straightened, nodding. To Weller, he said:

"I am satisfied Professor, that your invention does just as you claim. I don't see, however, how it could be used safely by our side as a war weapon. We couldn't put our enemies in soundproof chambers to kill them off, you know."

Weller chuckled. "Of course not. I will explain. Full-size vibrators would simply be dropped in enemy territory, with parachutes, by our airforce. Upon contact with the ground, they would automatically go into action. You've noticed the thickness of the enclosure walls necessary for safe use of the model vibrator. Imagine, then, the deadliness of one a dozen times as large and weighing three-hundred pounds! It would be effective for hundreds of yards. More effective than an atomic bomb—for where a bomb merely destroys, the vibrator would disintegrate utterly. And whereas the effects of a bomb last only for seconds, the vibrator would operate for periods as long as a half-hour."

"But when it stops…?" Major Calhern said. "What is to prevent our enemies from analyzing the vibrators, manufacturing them, and turning them upon us?"

WELLER looked smug. "I've taken care of that. When the vibrator stops, another automatic control would go into action, causing the device to explode."

"I see. And does the model contain such an automatic control?"

"No, it is far too small to contain the necessary parts." Weller became eager. "Well, Major Calhern, what is your opinion of the device?"

"Favorable, I assure you," Calhern responded. "Of course, more exhaustive tests will have to be made, using a full-size model, before the war department will consider using the invention. I will do everything within my power to see that you receive a proper hearing." Calhern glanced at his wristwatch. "And now I must leave to send in my report. You'll hear from me again in a few days."

Major Calhern shook hands with Arndt, Hollis, and myself, and then Professor Weller took him upstairs to show him out the door.

Arndt looked at the model vibrator on the workbench and growled deep in his throat. "Another and more deadly way of killing helpless people…as though we didn't have enough of that already! Makes me sick, just thinking of it. Well, I don't intend to stay and listen to that little egomaniac do further crowing over his invention." Arndt tugged his hat on his head with brisk, angry movements. "I'm leaving."

Hollis said abruptly, "I'm going with you. I have no desire to remain myself. Our colleague consistently forgot to mention that he developed the vibrator from one of my old ideas, and it would be a waste of time to demand credit where none is intended to be given."

They strode out of the laboratory, and their set faces left me with an unpleasant feeling of foreboding. When Professor Weller returned, his plump features were set in lines of anger.

"The stiff-necked, selfish fools," he snarled. "They're jealous, Kirk—*jealous*. Men of science...bah!" Abruptly he shrugged. "Well, I've showed them. You can leave, Kirk."

I met Gail on our usual corner at eight. Because of the fact that I worked for Professor Weller instead of her father, it was tacitly understood that I was none too welcome at her house. I'd have worked for Norman Hollis had he been able to pay me, but he couldn't, and he seemed to hold this fact against everyone, even including Gail. The life of an inventor is no bed of roses, and so I could hardly blame Weller for exulting in his moment of triumph. Hollis, I'm sure, would have done the same, just as Weller, too, would have been jealous and angry. That seems to be the way of life, and intelligent men are no exceptions.

Gail knew that her father had been present at Weller's demonstration, and she saw from my face that it had not come off quite as it should. She demanded to know what had happened. I explained reluctantly, going easy over the places where her father was concerned. But she was intuitive, and I knew my attempts at concealment hadn't been successful.

Gail was worried about her father, and what I had told her—or rather tried not to tell her—only served to make her more so. It had a dampening effect upon our evening.

We took in a movie at the largest of Groverton's two theatres, and then I saw Gail home. I lived with Professor Weller. It was about eleven-thirty when I got back.

I opened the door with my key. The light was on in the hall. The first thing I saw was Professor Weller. I almost stepped on him, in fact. He was lying there in the hall, just a few feet from the door, and he was very dead. The back of his skull was a mess of dried blood. A vicious blow on the head had killed him.

The horror of his silent figure held me motionless for a long moment. Then a sudden thought put me into motion, sent me running for the laboratory.

There could be only one reason for the murder of Professor Weller. The vibrator!

When I reached the laboratory, my eyes darted to the workbench, upon which I had last seen the invention. It was gone...

SHERIFF JOSHUA STROUD had his office in the Groverton courthouse. It was there that I found him, after having futilely telephoned his home and usual evening haunts. He explained he had been working late upon a case. I told him of Professor Weller's murder and the theft of the vibrator. He groaned and promised to come right up.

Sheriff Stroud arrived about twenty minutes later. With him were Bixby, his deputy, and Salter, the coroner. Groverton isn't a big town, in spite of the fact that it possesses a university. I guessed that Stroud's lateness was due to the necessity of routing his two assistants out of bed.

"Another murder," Stroud grumbled, gazing irascibly at the body of Professor Weller.

I stared at him in sudden apprehension. "Another murder?" I echoed. "What do you mean, Sheriff?" I was thinking of Hollis and Arndt.

"Found a dead man about three miles out of town this morning," Stroud explained. "Somebody shot him through the head. I haven't identified him yet . The person who killed him took all his papers, even ripped the labels out of his clothes."

Stroud shrugged and turned away. I wasn't fooled by his impatient, grumbling attitude. He had a reputation for being a relentless law hound who always got his man. There were quite a few sinister stories about his law enforcing methods, but there was no denying the fact that he always got results.

Salter stood up. Killed by a blow on the head. Some kind of blunt instrument. Dead about two hours."

"Two hours, eh?" Stroud said. He swung back to me. "Where were you, Rowan?"

"I was seeing a movie at the Ridge with Gail Hollis," I told him.

"What time was it that you last saw Weller alive?"

"About ten to eight."

"He was alone when you left him?"

"Yes." I added that the cooking and house-cleaning was done by Mrs. Guthrie, a neighbor. She lived a few doors down the block, communicating between her home and Weller's, as her duties required. She was seldom around in the evenings.

Stroud rubbed his studded jaw, his thin, dark face grim. "The way I see it, someone came to see Weller about an hour after you left. Weller let him in, then this person hit Weller over the head, killing him. You mentioned his invention being stolen over the telephone. That seems to have been the motive for the murder. Got any ideas about who may have done it, Rowan?"

I SHRUGGED. I told Stroud of the demonstration, which Professor Weller had given earlier in the evening, and of the three men who had been present, Major Calhern, Norman Hollis, and John Arndt. To my knowledge, only these three had known sufficient information about the invention to consider it worth murder and theft.

Stroud's black eyes lighted. "Hollis and Arndt... I happen to know these two were no particular friends of Weller's—especially Hollis. I'm pretty sure one of the two murdered him."

Stroud made an examination of the house and laboratory. He found nothing, however, and presently led his two yawning assistants away. Later, the men from the undertaker's arrived, and Professor Weller's remains were carried out.

There was no sleep for me. I spent the greater part of the night chain-smoking and pacing the floor.

A little after eleven the next morning, Sheriff Stroud was back at the house. His presence came as a relief to me. Mrs. Guthrie was afraid of him, as were many in Groverton, and she left when he came. She had been plaguing me with questions all morning, doubtless to arm herself with gossip to regale her curious friends. I could very easily imagine how news of Professor Weller's murder must have fired Groverton.

"Learn anything?" I asked Stroud.

He shrugged. "I questioned Hollis and Arndt, and they let me search their places. If either of them has the invention, it isn't where you can find it very easily. Arndt claims to have been home all last night, and his housekeeper, that Harrick woman, vouches for him. I think you've heard some of the rumors about Arndt and Susan Harrick. They live like man and wife, if you're willing to believe gossip. They might be lying—but how can I prove it?

"As for Hollis, he was home alone, what with Gail gone to the movies with you. Hollis says he didn't set foot out of the house all evening. He might have come here and murdered Weller, but there's no slightest bit of evidence.

"I checked on that Major Calhern, too. Washington sent him here to Groverton, all right. And the night clerk at the hotel says Calhern came in about seven-thirty and stayed in all evening. That leaves Hollis and Arndt. Rowan, I'm convinced that one of the two murdered Weller and stole his invention. Somehow, I've got to find out which one it was..." His voice grew grim. "There must he some way!"

There was a long period of silence, during which Stroud stared into space, his dark brows knitted fiercely. More to break the silence than anything else, I told him that I had discovered something else. In going through the laboratory that morning, I had found that Professor Weller's records had undergone a hasty search. Every piece of paper relating to the vibrator had been taken.

"The laboratory..." Stroud said musingly. "Let's go down there, Rowan."

The laboratory looked ghostly in such of the morning sunlight as managed to filter in through the few grimy windows. I switched on the lights, and Stroud looked around. He asked:

"Where was the invention when you saw it last, Rowan?"

I pointed mutely at the workbench.

"An easy matter to find it, then," Stroud muttered. "Look," he said abruptly, "how did Weller's invention work? What did it do?"

EXPLANATION of the operating principle of the vibrator would have gone over Stroud's head. I merely told him that the device emitted ultra high-frequency vibrations capable of disintegrating glass and stone, and also of destroying the delicate tissues of the brain in human beings. Because of its deadliness, the vibrator could never be operated, except within the thick, specially-constructed confines of the test chamber. Turning it on and off was accomplished by remote control.

Stroud gazed keenly at me as I finished. "Remote control? How do you mean, Rowan? Wires, or something like that?"

"Radio," I explained. I indicated the control board. "That's basically a radio transmitter. It's quite powerful."

Stroud was suddenly tense. "How powerful, Rowan? Powerful enough to reach across Groverton?"

I gasped, "Good Lord—yes!" And then I stared at him. And as I stared, I recalled all the unsavory stories I had heard about the ruthless means whereby he had served the ends of justice. I realized now what he meant to do. Whoever had killed Professor Weller still had the vibrator. And the device, wherever it was now, could be put into action by the radio transmitter!

It would reveal one of two things—or both. It would destroy its hiding place, thus indicating the location of the murderer of Professor Weller. Or, if the murderer were near enough, it would destroy him, too.

Thus, after the vibrator had been put into action, a simple check would solve the case. I said as much to Stroud.

"Exactly," he said softly. His black eyes were intense upon mine.

"But that's hardly legal," I protested. "What you mean to do would be equivalent to an unofficial death sentence."

Stroud made a curt gesture of impatience. "Don't be a hidebound fool, Rowan. We're dealing with a murderer— someone who must pay the penalty for his crime. This is the only way we have of finding him and getting evidence against him. Using ordinary legal methods, I'd be helpless. I haven't a shred of proof against anyone."

"I won't do it," I snapped. And I knew why I wouldn't do it. I was very much afraid that the person who had killed Professor Weller and stolen his invention was Norman Hollis. Everything pointed to the man. He had hated Weller, feeling as he did that the vibrator was the result of one of his own ideas, a debt for which Weller hadn't given him the slightest bit of credit. And he had been envious of Weller's accomplishment, jealous of the fame it would bring the other. Hollis had been alone all evening. He might very well have come to the house, killed Weller, and stolen the invention...

But he was Gail's father—and I loved Gail. Suppose he were really the murderer...suppose he were near the vibrator when I caused it to operate by means of the transmitter—his death would be on my hands. And murderer or not, Gail would blame me for the death of her father. She wouldn't marry a man with her father's blood on his hands...

IT WAS a nasty situation. The more I thought about it, the less I liked it. Operating that transmitter might very well solve the case for Stroud—but it would sure as hell complicate my own case. It would spoil all my hopes and plans where Gail was concerned.

Stroud shifted impatiently. His black eyes were cold. "Rowan, this is my only chance to solve the case. I tell you, I won't be balked!"

"I won't do it," I muttered. "I just can't do it."

"And why, Rowan? What're you afraid of? Do you know who the murderer is? You wouldn't like to have him die?"

I shook my head dumbly.

Stroud exploded, "By God, Rowan, if you won't operate that radio, I'll do it myself!"

"You don't know how," I said.

"You could show me how."

"You'll have to force me."

Stroud brought his thin, dark face close to mine. His black eyes blazed at me. "I'll do just that. Rowan, remember I'm the Law. I've got the power to command."

"Not in this case," I snapped. "It isn't legal. You may be the Law—but your authority doesn't possess the powers of judge, jury, and executioner. You're sentencing a man to death without first bringing him to trial."

"You're a fool," Stroud flamed. "How can you be sure the murderer will be anywhere near the invention when you operate the radio? And as for bringing him to trial—haven't I explained that's impossible? I haven't the slightest bit of proof against anyone." His eyes narrowed, and his voice became deadly soft. "Rowan, you're obstructing justice. I could have you up for that... Or, Rowan, I could fix it so that you'd get the blame for Weller's murder. Don't doubt it an instant. I've got to get a murderer, and if I can't get the real one, you'll do."

And Stroud meant it, I knew. Every word of it.

I was trapped—and there was no way out. There was nothing I could do but what Stroud wanted me to do.

I shrugged my shoulders wearily and nodded. "I give in," I said.

Stroud's smile was thin and hard. "Good! Let's get to work at once."

"Wait," I said. "I want to call up Gail Hollis, to get her out of the house."

"So that's the answer, eh?" Stroud exclaimed. "You're sure Norman Hollis is the murderer. You're afraid the girl will get hurt if the invention happens to be hidden in the house... All right, you can call her—but no tricks, Rowan. Don't try to warn Hollis."

Stroud accompanied me to the telephone, and his glittering black eyes watched me every second I spoke. My ruse was a simple one. I merely told Gail to meet me at our usual corner, that it was important. I didn't explain. I told her that, and then I hung up.

I GOT to work upon the radio transmitter, making the adjustments necessary to reach the vibrator. Then I was ready. I breathed a silent prayer for Gail, and I breathed a silent prayer for myself. And I hoped against hope that Norman Hollis, if he had the vibrator, wouldn't be within its deadly range.

I threw in the switch.

Stroud demanded, "It's done?"

I nodded like a puppet. I couldn't speak. I felt as though I'd never be able to speak again.

Lips pressed against his teeth in a wolfish grin, eyes glittering like bits of polished jet, Stroud ran from the laboratory. I sat down and stared into empty space. I was afraid to think.

How much later it was when I heard the doorbell ring, I don't know. It roused me from my apathy. I went up to open the door.

Gail stumbled into my arms. "Kirk! What's wrong? You sounded so queer over the telephone... And I waited at the corner, and you didn't come. I got worried and rushed over here." She searched my face anxiously. "Kirk, what is it? What has happened?"

I couldn't bring myself to explain. I was afraid to tell her what I had done—afraid to tell her that her father might be dead even now, and that I was the one responsible.

Gail clutched at my arms. "Kirk—what is it? Why don't you tell me?"

I gulped my voice into action. "I can't tell you, honey," I said. "Stroud and I are working on something, which may solve the mystery of Professor Weller's death. We've got to wait until Stroud comes back. Then you'll know."

Gail looked doubtful, but she desisted from questioning me. She went into the kitchen and made coffee. It was good coffee—but I didn't notice that then. I was thinking furiously.

Hollis. Was the murderer Hollis? Was he dead now—or still alive? I hoped desperately that he was still alive.

Or Arndt. Arndt might very well be the murderer. I prayed that it would be Arndt.

The afternoon wore away with infinite slowness. The suspense of waiting, not knowing, almost drove me mad.

And then—at long last—there was the sound of a car stopping before the house. Gail and I rushed to the door as Sheriff Stroud burst in.

"Well, the case is solved," Stroud announced triumphantly. "I've caught the murderer of Professor Weller. It worked beautifully, Rowan."

"Who—who was it?" I husked.

"Calhern," Stroud replied.

I WENT weak with relief. My legs became so rubbery, I had to sit down in a chair. The next instant implications of the name hit me, and I bounced up with a cry of protest.

"But that's impossible," I yelped. "Calhern couldn't have been the murderer. Why—why, he had been sent from Washington by the war department. He wouldn't do a thing like that!"

"But he did, Rowan." Stroud's grin broadened. "You see, Calhern wasn't Calhern at all, but an immensely clever international spy masquerading as Calhern. The real Calhern was the unidentified dead man I found outside of town yesterday morning!"

I sat down in the chair again.

Stroud went on, "What obviously happened is this. Somehow the spy learned about the real Major Calhern's mission. He intercepted Calhern on the outskirts of Groverton. Probably, he forced Calhern's car into the ditch, then shot Calhern, and exchanged his clothes for Calhern's uniform, ripping out the labels as he did so. Then he drove on into town, a confederate driving away Calhern's own car.

"The spy wanted Professor Weller's invention. Our enemies would gladly have given him a fortune for a thing like that at this time. He attended Professor Weller's demonstration, learning all that he wanted to know. Then, later in the evening, he slipped out of the hotel, went to Weller's house, and killed him, taking the invention and all the notes relating to it.

"The spy's room was on the second floor. It would have been an easy matter to run a rope out of the window, thus getting in and out without the night clerk seeing him. The vibrator itself he had left in his car."

"But how did you catch him?" I demanded. "How did you find out?"

"I didn't catch him," Stroud said. "The vibrator did. We used the radio just in time. The spy was leaving town. He was about a mile out when the invention went into action. His car crashed into a tree. There wasn't much left of him, but from the papers in the uniform he wore, I found out all I needed to know."

Stroud grinned and started for the door. "Well, that's that. I've still got some work to do, though." He grinned again, waved at us, and left.

I bounced out of the chair. Gail never knew why I yelled with joy. She still doesn't know why I hugged her so hard.

## THE END

*If you've enjoyed this book, you will not want to miss these terrific titles...*

## ARMCHAIR SCI-FI & HORROR DOUBLE NOVELS, $12.95 each

**D-1**    **THE GALAXY RAIDERS** by William P. McGivern
       **SPACE STATION #1** by Frank Belknap Long

**D-2**    **THE PROGRAMMED PEOPLE** by Jack Sharkey
       **SLAVES OF THE CRYSTAL BRAIN** by William Carter Sawtelle

**D-3**    **YOU'RE ALL ALONE** by Fritz Leiber
       **THE LIQUID MAN** by Bernard C. Gilford

**D-4**    **CITADEL OF THE STAR LORDS** by Edmond Hamilton
       **VOYAGE TO ETERNITY** by Milton Lesser

**D-5**    **IRON MEN OF VENUS** by Don Wilcox
       **THE MAN WITH ABSOLUTE MOTION** by Noel Loomis

**D-6**    **WHO SOWS THE WIND...** by Rog Phillips
       **THE PUZZLE PLANET** by Robert A. W. Lowndes

**D-7**    **PLANET OF DREAD** by Murray Leinster
       **TWICE UPON A TIME** by Charles L. Fontenay

**D-8**    **THE TERROR OUT OF SPACE** by Dwight V. Swain
       **QUEST OF THE GOLDEN APE** by Ivar Jorgensen and Adam Chase

**D-9**    **SECRET OF MARRACOTT DEEP** by Henry Slesar
       **PAWN OF THE BLACK FLEET** by Mark Clifton.

**D-10**    **BEYOND THE RINGS OF SATURN** by Robert Moore Williams
       **A MAN OBSESSED** by Alan E. Nourse

## ARMCHAIR SCIENCE FICTION CLASSICS, $12.95 each

**C-1**    **THE GREEN MAN**
       by Harold M. Sherman

**C-2**    **A TRACE OF MEMORY**
       By Keith Laumer

**C-3**    **INTO PLUTONIAN DEPTHS**
       by Stanton A. Coblentz

## ARMCHAIR MASTERS OF SCIENCE FICTION SERIES, $16.95 each

**M-1**    **MASTERS OF SCIENCE FICTION, Vol. One**
       Bryce Walton—"Dark of the Moon" and other tales

**M-2**    **MASTERS OF SCIENCE FICTION, Vol. Two**
       Jerome Bixby—"One Way Street" and other tales

*If you've enjoyed this book, you will not want to miss these terrific titles…*